Back Home Again

Tales from Grace Chapel Inn™

Back Home Again

MELODY CARLSON

GuidepostsBooks™

New York, New York

Back Home Again

ISBN 0-8249-4700-2

Published by GuidepostsBooks
16 East 34th Street,
New York, New York 10016
www.guidepostsbooks.com

Distributed by Ideals Publications, a Guideposts company
535 Metroplex Drive, Suite 250
Nashville, Tennessee 37211

GuidepostsBooks, *Ideals*, and *Tales from Grace Chapel Inn* are registered
trademarks of Guideposts, Carmel, New York.

Library of Congress Cataloging-in-Publication Data

Carlson, Melody.
  Back home again / Melody Carlson.
      p. cm. — (Tales from Grace Chapel Inn)
  ISBN 0-8249-4700-2
  1. Sisters—Fiction. 2. Bed and breakfast accommodations—Fiction. 3.
Pennsylvania—Fiction. I. Title. II. Series.
  PS3553.A73257B33 2006
  813'.54—dc22
                        2006005583

Cover illustration by Deborah Chabrian
Designed by Marisa Jackson

Printed and bound in the United States of America

10   9   8   7   6   5   4   3   2   1

GRACE CHAPEL INN

A place where one can be
refreshed and encouraged,
a place of hope and healing,
a place where God is at home.

Chapter One

*T*hin rays of afternoon sunlight filtered through the leaves of the old maple tree that dominated the front yard of the Howard family home. Unshed tears blurred Alice Howard's vision as she squinted up at the tree's majestic canopy. How was it possible that more than fifty years had passed since her father had dug a gallon-sized hole and planted that spindly twig? Yet she remembered the day as if it were yesterday. Father had planted the tree for two reasons: first, to celebrate the birth of his third daughter Jane; and second, to honor the memory of his beloved wife Madeleine. As a result, the tree had always evoked mixed feelings in Alice. She had dearly loved her little sister, but like any normal twelve-year-old girl, she had also mourned the loss of her mother.

And now Father was gone too. For the first time, the reality of this loss penetrated her heart like a well-aimed sword, and her tears began to fall freely. It had been such a shock to receive that phone call today at work. Her father had seemed perfectly fine earlier that morning. Fred

Humbert was the one to call. He explained how he'd left his hardware store to take a look at the leaky kitchen faucet that her father had told him about yesterday. He had knocked several times before he let himself in.

"I found him sitting in his chair in the study, Alice, just like he'd peacefully gone to sleep. But when I tapped him on the shoulder, I knew something was wrong. I guess he'd had a heart attack. I could tell he was gone. Probably had been for a couple of hours. I knew it was no use to call the paramedics, so I decided to call you. I figured you'd know what to do."

Alice had sped home and had spent the rest of the day dealing with *things*. Now that the arrangements had been made and her two sisters had been notified, there seemed to be little left to do, other than to wait.

It was the waiting that undid her. All she could think of was Father and all the little things she would miss about him, like his sunny smile, and the way he liked to sneak table scraps to Wendell and then complain that the cat was getting too chubby. She would miss his reading aloud to her from the local weekly newspaper and the way he added his own editorial comments that never failed to make her chuckle. No, life would never be the same again.

Of course, Father had been quite old and his health had been failing for years, but Alice had never really pre-pared herself for the reality of his actual absence. Perhaps she'd been in denial. There was no denying it now. He was gone, and there was a big hole in her life. She sat down on the creaky front porch swing next to Wendell. With a deep sigh, she ran her hand over his warm, gray and black fur and wondered what was going on in that feline brain right now. Did he know what had happened this morning? Of course, he must. After all, Father had always claimed that Wendell was "insightful—for a cat anyway." She scratched his favorite spot, on the top of his head right between his ears, and continued to wait. Oh, if only Louise and Jane would get here.

"Alice!" called a shrill voice from behind her. "Alice Christine, where *are* you?"

Alice glanced toward the north side of the house in time to spy a flash of vivid red hair just passing through the overgrown rose trellis. She recognized the shade as "Titian Dreams"—the color that Aunt Ethel's hairdresser applied to her roots every four weeks. Alice knew she might be able to avoid Aunt Ethel if she hurried into the house, but what would be the use? Her aunt would eventually catch up with her anyway. For, despite Aunt Ethel's age (which Alice suspected was mid-seventies, although Aunt Ethel kept this secret) she was a sharp old woman, both in wit and in tongue. And during the ten years she'd lived in the carriage house next door, she'd become one of Alice's greatest challenges in life.

It had been Father's suggestion to relocate Aunt Ethel nearby. He had been concerned about his younger sister's growing old alone, and at the time it sounded like a good idea to Alice too. She'd envisioned the three of them becoming a sort of family. And indeed they had in their own way.

"I'm on the porch," Alice called.

"Oh, Alice! What are you doing just sitting around at a time like this? Land sakes, there must be a hundred things to do right now."

"Yes," Alice said with a tired smile. "And I've been doing them."

"But I was just chatting with Carlene Moss down at the newspaper, and she said that you hadn't notified them of Daniel's demise yet. Naturally, they'll want to do a front-page story about Daniel's life of service here in Acorn Hill—probably need a good photograph too. I think I may have one that will work. Goodness knows that man gave his life to his congregation. For more than six decades too! And what about the memorial service, Alice, have you decided what to—"

"I thought I'd leave some decisions until Jane and Louise arrive."

"And when might that be?" Aunt Ethel peered down at her watch as if she were the stationmaster waiting for a delayed train.

Alice shrugged. "I'm not sure, but I'm guessing Louise might arrive later this afternoon and Jane by tomorrow evening."

"Well, I guess it's all right for you to sit around all day long if you like, but I have places to go, people to see."

Alice stood up. Leaning over the porch railing she peered into her aunt's pale blue eyes. "But don't you miss him, Auntie?"

For a brief moment, Aunt Ethel's veneer of busyness and efficiency seemed to crack slightly, and she even sniffed. "Well, of course, I miss him, dear. He was my only living brother, and I expected him to go on forever." She now pulled a lace-trimmed hanky from the bodice of her floral dress and dabbed her nose. "I just don't have time to dwell on it right now."

Alice partially understood her aunt's philosophy. Sometimes it was easier to keep yourself busy and distracted, to hold your emotions at bay. But maybe it wasn't always the best route—at least not in the long run.

"What about this old house?" demanded the aunt, changing the subject as only she could do. "Didn't your father leave this place to the chapel? Does that mean you'll be moving out soon?"

Alice slowly shook her head. "Actually Father left it to us—to Jane and Louise and me."

Aunt Ethel frowned as if this were the silliest plan imaginable. "What on earth will the three of you do with this house? Good gracious, it's falling down around your ears."

"I don't know what we'll do with it, but Father had been going on about this idea quite a lot recently. He recalled when we three girls were growing up here. He kept reminding me of all the good times we'd shared in this house. I think he hoped that giving it to us would somehow help to bring us back together again."

Aunt Ethel laughed, but there was a distinct note of sarcasm in it. "Well, now wouldn't *that* be something. I'll tell you what, Alice, I've never, not in all my born days, ever known flesh-and-blood sisters any less alike than you three."

Alice knew her aunt was mostly right, but the tactless comment still irked her. Yet, she kept her reaction to herself.

"Well, you three would be wise to sell off this rundown old place quickly before it deteriorates even more. *Tsk-tsk.* Just look at that peeling paint."

Alice stroked Wendell's coat more firmly than before. The cat reacted by hopping down and sashaying across the porch.

"Oh, there's Lloyd," said Aunt Ethel suddenly. She waved across the street, and then called out a chirpy *"Yoo-hoo!"*

Lloyd Tynan had on his light blue seersucker suit today, with a darker blue shirt and a crisp white bowtie. He smiled broadly and waved back. As mayor of Acorn Hill, not to mention Aunt Ethel's most recent beau, it was likely he had already heard the sad news. And, if not, he would certainly hear about it now.

"Will you excuse me, dear?" Aunt Ethel gave her flamboyant coiffure a quick little pat. "I need to go speak to Lloyd about something I'd like him to say at your father's service."

"Not at all." Alice felt a wave of relief pass over her. Thank goodness for Lloyd. If he hadn't shown up at that moment, she might have been subjected to another one of Aunt Ethel's little lectures on why Alice should get herself married, particularly now that her father was gone. This was one of her aunt's favorite topics and could always be counted on at times of weddings, births, showers, holidays, or funerals. Alice's age of sixty-two did nothing to deter her aunt either. Everyone in town knew that Aunt Ethel firmly believed that romance wasn't limited to the young.

Just the same, Alice was certain she didn't have it in her to abide that particular speech. Not today anyway. Long ago, Alice had resigned herself to her single lifestyle. She enjoyed nursing and caring for others, and she devoted herself to her youth group and really loved those girls as if they were her own. What did it matter if they were young enough to be her grandchildren now?

Father had always provided a good buffer for Aunt Ethel's thoughtless interference, lovingly reminding Alice how useful and helpful she was to so many. He enjoyed replaying the occasional story he heard at the coffee shop (although she was certain he exaggerated) about the various patients who were "touched by Alice's selfless kindnesses" during their hospital stays—as if she were some kind of Florence Nightingale. Father would remind her of the importance of her work with the young girls in the church. It had all helped to balance things out. But now that he was gone, Aunt Ethel had the upper hand.

Alice walked down the porch steps, treading gently on the board that was loose, as she peered down the quiet street toward town. The pavement shimmered like wavy glass in the hot afternoon sun. Would this summer never end? It was September already, and yet just as hot as mid-July. She stepped onto the sidewalk and looked toward Hill Street, longing to see Louise's car turning the corner at the four-way stop before it slowly proceeded this way. But Chapel Road remained just as quiet and empty as the old Victorian house behind her.

Chapter Two

Alice forced herself to go back inside the house. She knew that time would pass more quickly if she kept busy, but the old house felt so big and empty now, so silent. Father had not been a noisy person, but his absence seemed like a physical vacuum to her, as if there now existed a gaping void that she could actually sense. She didn't mean this in a supernatural or frightening way; certainly Alice didn't believe in ghosts. She had no doubts that Father was securely in heaven right now, but still there was something perplexing about his not being here anymore.

"Shake it off," she chided herself as she stooped down to straighten the old wine and navy oriental carpet in the foyer, pausing to notice how the finish on the parquet floor was worn thin. She stood up and took in a deep breath. "Just shake it off." This was an admonition she sometimes used in her nursing work, during those rare but difficult moments when caring for a burn patient or a child who'd suffered abuse or neglect. It was her reminder to put aside her personal feelings and give her very best to her patients.

Naturally she would pray during these times too. Prayer was a real lifeline for Alice. She had been praying on and off again ever since this morning's phone call. It was the only thing that had helped her to get through.

She walked from room to room now, looking more closely at her family home than she had done in ages. Everything here was so familiar to her that she almost didn't see it anymore. She rarely noticed things like faded gold velvet drapery that probably needed cleaning, or the old sagging brown mohair sofa where Wendell had sharpened his claws a few times too many. She usually looked past the peeling wallpaper with its sad-looking yellow flowers that had once been bright and cheerful. Of course, she knew the house was run down, but it was a friendly sort of wornness, like a pair of old slippers that had been properly broken in, or so it seemed to her. She wasn't too sure about how it would appear to her sisters.

It had been several years since Louise and Jane had been back here at the same time. With her siblings' work and their personal crises, it had been nearly impossible to schedule a time when they could all reunite. Most recently, Jane had been tied up in a painful divorce and running a restaurant. And Louise always had her piano students, an active social life, as well as accompanying for the occasional concert for her church or music community. Always there was one reason or another not to come home to see

Father. And now it was too late. Alice felt certain her sisters would feel bad about this, but she also knew that her father understood perfectly.

She wondered what Jane and Louise would think of the family home. Would they, like Aunt Ethel, see it as a decrepit old place that would be better off sold to the highest bidder? She doubted that anyone would pay much for the house in its current condition. But what about Father's wishes? What about honoring his last requests? What would her sisters think about that?

Alice paused in the dining room as she caught sight of her reflection in the large oak-framed mirror above the sideboard. Was that old woman really her? She peered at her image, shaking her head at her worry-creased brow. Like the family home, she looked tired and worn. She wondered if she should do something to improve her appearance before Louise arrived. She still had on her nurse's uniform, serviceable and comfortable, but probably not her most attractive outfit. She suddenly remembered Louise's comments the first time she saw Alice dressed like this.

"White is definitely *not* your best color, dear," Louise had said with the authority of an older sister who always managed to dress impeccably. "It completely washes you out. Too bad they don't have uniforms in a nice peach shade. That would look well with your reddish hair."

Alice's hair had been a light auburn back in her younger days. Now it was faded to a hue of rusty driftwood. Not an unpleasant color really, and some people even thought it went nicely with her golden brown eyes. She'd worn her hair short since her forties because it was low maintenance and the natural curl seemed to frame her face, or so Betty at the hair salon said.

"Short hair gives your face a real lift," Betty assured Alice each time she put away her cutting shears. "And you have such beautiful skin, hardly a wrinkle. I'll bet you can still pass for fifty."

Alice always laughed at such nonsense. Yet at the same time, she found it hard to believe that she was really sixty-two. How could that be? When did it happen? Equally amazing was the fact that her baby sister was actually fifty now. A new ripple of nervous anticipation coursed through her as she remembered that both sisters would soon be here.

Just then she heard a "yoo-hoo." It sounded similar to Aunt Ethel's greeting, but slightly different, a lower note perhaps.

"Louise?" she called out expectantly as she hurried toward the front door. "Is that you?"

There in the open doorway stood Louise with a pastel blue and taupe tapestry overnight bag over one arm and a neat leather purse on the other. She looked older with more white in her gray hair, and slightly plumper than before, but she was definitely Louise, wearing the same classic single strand of pearls and her sweater set. Today it was baby blue, the same shade as her eyes. And her skirt was a sedate tone of beige that perfectly matched her purse and sensible low-heeled pumps.

"Alice!" she cried as she dropped the overnight bag and held out her arms.

"Oh, Louise!" Alice ran toward her sister and hugged her. "It's so good to have you here."

The two held each other for a few moments, and Alice could feel fresh tears spilling down her face. In some ways Louise had been like a mother to her. Even though they hadn't always agreed on everything back then or even now, Louise had always been there for Alice. And here she was now.

Finally Alice stepped back and searched her pocket for a tissue. Unable to find one, she looked up to see Louise holding out a neatly pressed linen handkerchief with a lacy blue *L* embroidered on the corner. "Here you go, dear," said Louise with a faint smile. "You never were one to have a hanky when you needed it."

Alice smiled and took the handkerchief and dried her cheeks. "No. I guess I haven't changed much in that regard."

Louise seemed to be studying her now. "But you have definitely changed, dear. Goodness sakes, we *are* getting older, aren't we?"

Alice sniffed and nodded. "Yes, I was just thinking that same thing a few minutes ago. I can't figure out how it happened so quickly. Doesn't it seem like only yesterday that we were playing house in the backyard? Fixing tea parties for our dolls and making kites out of newspaper and string?"

Louise nodded. "It seems those memories from my childhood grow more vivid with each passing year. We had a lovely childhood, didn't we, Alice? Other than losing Mother, that is. Other than that, it was nice, wasn't it?"

"It was." Alice reached down and picked up Louise's tapestry bag. "Everything happened so fast that I haven't had a chance to do much more than freshen the sheets on your bed. I'm afraid it's a little dusty up there. I did open the window to air it out a bit."

"Don't worry about a thing. I'll just make myself at home and clean anything as needed. I certainly don't expect you to be my maid. Goodness knows you've probably been terribly busy what with making arrangements and all. There are so many decisions to make. It wasn't too many years ago that I had to do all this for Eliot. How are you holding up, dear?"

Alice shrugged. "Okay, I guess. I mean, it's still just sinking in. I can't quite believe he's really gone."

"I know." Louise sadly shook her head. "Father was such a rock, like an institution in this town . . . I'm sure I thought he would simply live on and on forever—on earth I mean.

Of course, I realize that he's alive in heaven right now. That's some comfort, isn't it?"

"Yes, but I still miss him."

"I'm sure you do, dear." Louise reached over and gave her arm a squeeze. "At least you got to enjoy his final years with him. Now that's something, isn't it?"

"Yes. I don't regret that at all." Alice dabbed at her eyes again. "Do you have more bags in the car, Louise?"

"Yes. Just one, but it's a little heavy."

Squaring her shoulders, Alice stood straighter. "No problem. If I can still hoist a two-hundred-pound patient, I'm sure I can handle your bag. Why don't you go get yourself settled, and I'll go get it for you."

"Thank you, dear." Louise handed her the car keys.

Alice went out to see Louise's car parked in front. It was the same white Cadillac she'd been driving for more than two decades, yet it still looked in perfect condition. It wasn't old enough to be an antique yet, but perhaps in time. It was comforting the way some things always stayed the same. Louise seemed like that, unchangeable, unflappable, predictable and dependable. Alice felt relieved that her sister was here. She opened the trunk and retrieved the large bag and wheeled it up the walk to the house. It didn't seem so terribly heavy at first, but by the time she'd lugged it up the stairs she was breathing harder.

"I'm in here, dear," called Louise from her old bedroom.

Alice paused to catch her breath, then wheeled the bag into Louise's room. "Everything okay in here?"

"It's wonderful—just the same as ever. I'm so glad you didn't change a thing."

Alice wiped her finger through the dust on the dresser and frowned. "Not even the dust."

"Don't you worry, I'll get rid of that in no time." Louise removed several prescription bottles and set them down on the dresser. "My doctor has me taking all sorts of pills these days—some for my bones and my blood pressure and goodness knows what else."

Alice smiled. "Guess that's what happens when we get old. I used to have the hardest time getting Father to take his pills regularly. He was always forgetting. Finally I made him start using one of those boxes with all the days of the week on it."

"I've been meaning to get one of those for myself."

"Well, don't bother. You can have his—" Suddenly Alice began to tear up again.

"I'm sorry, dear." Louise came over and put an arm around her shoulders. "This has really been hard on you, hasn't it?"

Alice nodded. "I'd better go see to some things in the kitchen, Louise. I'm sure you'll be hungry for dinner soon."

"Do you know when Jane will arrive?"

"She can't get a flight out of San Francisco until tomorrow."

Louise smiled. "Oh, I can't wait to see her! How is she doing? Did she say much about the restaurant?"

"Not really. It was a quick conversation. We can catch up when she gets here. I think she said that her flight would arrive by tomorrow afternoon, around five."

"It's just like a family reunion, isn't it?"

"Sort of." Alice hesitated, and then added in a quavering voice, "Except for Father."

Louise nodded. "Well, he's here in spirit, Alice. I'm sure he's smiling down on us right now, happy to see us back together again."

"Yes. I'm sure he is." Even so, Alice thought it would have been nicer if Father had been here with them, in person.

Chapter Three

After a quiet breakfast with Louise the next morning, Alice spent several hours straightening and organizing the kitchen while Louise made some phone calls. Alice enjoyed the distraction and hoped to get the kitchen whipped into shape before the day became too busy. She remembered how fastidious Jane was about cooking spaces, and Alice feared that she had allowed theirs to get a bit shabby lately. It wasn't completely her fault, because Father often shooed her off to work in the mornings, assuring her that he would clean up their breakfast things. But his ideas of cleaning weren't always the same as hers. Still, she had always appreciated his willingness to help out and never would have dreamed of criticizing. It usually turned out that by the time she came home to fix dinner, she was often tired or in a hurry to get to a meeting, and, well, sometimes things just went undone.

She'd been a bit embarrassed yesterday when the first of the women had started slipping food items into their ancient refrigerator. It hadn't been thoroughly wiped down in ages. She supposed she should have been better prepared, knowing how the women at Grace Chapel always reacted like this whenever someone in their congregation passed away. It was as if they derived a sense of comfort and well-being as they carefully prepared their casseroles, baked goods and gelatin salads for the grieving family. They were probably also relieved not to be the ones on the receiving end. Alice knew that feeling from personal experience. Her standard contribution at times of bereavement was usually macaroni salad. How many times had she concocted that salad, thankful that she had escaped being the recipient of the culinary gifts? Well, no one could escape it forever.

By noon, Alice decided to call it good in the kitchen. She pulled out several of the prepared dishes from the refrigerator and attempted to set the table for a simple lunch.

"*Yoo-hoo!*" called a shrill voice from the front foyer. "Alice, are you here?"

"I'm in the kitchen, Aunt Ethel," Alice called out. "Coming."

Alice met Aunt Ethel in the dining room. Her aunt smiled brightly as she held out a large glass baking dish covered in aluminum foil. "I saw Fred in the hardware store and he asked me to drop this apple cobbler by. Vera baked it early this morning but didn't have time to bring it by before school started."

The smell of cinnamon wafted up as Alice took the heavy dish from her aunt. "How sweet of her. Thank you for bringing it by."

"Is that Louise's car parked out front?" asked Ethel as she pushed open the swinging doors to the kitchen and peered curiously about.

"Yes, she arrived last night."

"Oh, goody." Aunt Ethel clapped her hands like a little girl. "Where is she now?"

"I believe she's in her room."

"Well, I'll just run up and say a quick hello."

Alice smiled to herself as she wondered if Aunt Ethel had *ever* said a "quick" hello. She set the cobbler on the butcher-block counter and finished working on her lunch preparations.

"Hello in the house," called another female voice. This time it came from the back porch.

"Hope," Alice exclaimed. "I didn't expect to find you on my back porch."

Hope Collins smiled sadly. "We heard the news about Pastor Daniel yesterday. We all felt so bad down at the Coffee Shop that we decided to send over his favorite treat."

Alice nodded. "Blackberry pie."

Hope handed her the still warm pie. "I'm sure you've been deluged with food already."

"But no blackberry pie."

"Well, it's just our way of saying how much we loved that man." Hope wiped a tear that left a dark mascara smudge on her cheek.

Alice gave Hope's hand a gentle squeeze. "Father really enjoyed his little visits with you at the Coffee Shop."

Hope shook her head. "Not nearly as much as I did. I'm sure going to miss him."

Alice sighed. "I miss him too, Hope. I mean I realize that Father was quite old and I know he was ready to go at anytime, but I still can't completely believe he's gone. Even this morning I got up and started to make him a pot of coffee."

"I know what you mean. Yesterday afternoon, when it got to the time he usually dropped by, I had to remind myself he wasn't coming in. It's odd. Just this week he gave me a little book to read about faith growing in times of trial. I was too busy to get to it before, but I'll make sure I do now."

Alice remembered how Father had asked her to pray for Hope. He believed she had a genuinely searching heart. "Well, if you ever want to talk about the book with someone . . ." Alice smiled hopefully. "I'd be happy to do that with you."

"Oh, that would be so nice. Maybe you could stop in, and we could discuss it."

"Yes, definitely. I'll plan on it."

Hope pushed a stray lock of light brown hair from her eyes. "I better be getting back now. I promised to only be gone a few minutes."

"Thanks, Hope. For everything."

Alice could hear Louise and Aunt Ethel talking as she went back into the house. Aunt Ethel was already filling Louise in on all the latest Acorn Hill gossip. "And you remember Lloyd Tynan, don't you? I think he was a few years ahead of you in school. Well, maybe you hadn't heard that he's the mayor now, he retired from his business a few years back and then decided he could do a far better job of running this town than old Billy Thorpe. Billy was a big talker, but lazier than all get out." Aunt Ethel paused for a breath when Alice walked in.

"Alice," said Louise with what appeared to be sincere relief, "who was at the door?"

"That was Hope from the Coffee Shop. She dropped by a blackberry pie, Father's favorite."

"Did I notice you fixing some lunch?" asked Aunt Ethel.

"Yes." Alice smiled ruefully at Louise. "Would you like to join us?"

Naturally, Aunt Ethel would like nothing better. After a light lunch, while Aunt Ethel and Louise continued to visit, Alice busied herself by mixing up some hand-squeezed lemonade. Father had always enjoyed a glass of ice-cold lemonade on a hot afternoon, and according to the thermometer, just outside the kitchen window, it was nearly eighty degrees already.

She was just stirring in the sugar when Louise popped into the kitchen.

"Why, Alice Christine, is that homemade lemonade you've got there?" asked Louise.

Alice nodded as she proudly held out the pitcher. "Yep. Just what the doctor ordered."

Aunt Ethel slipped in behind Louise now. "Why, that sounds perfectly lovely, Alice." Then she took Louise by the arm. "And it's a perfectly lovely day for it. Why don't we enjoy it out on the front porch."

Alice took her time filling the tall glasses with ice cubes and lemonade, arranging them on the tray with dainty pink napkins and a small plate of the sugar cookies that Patsy Ley had dropped by earlier. Patsy's husband Henry was the associate pastor at Grace Chapel, but why Father had ever hired the soft-spoken man was something of a mystery. Henry had a good heart and was a natural listener, but because of his stammering speech, he found preaching a real trial. As a result, Father had continued fulfilling this role in the pulpit. Now that she thought about it, perhaps *that* was exactly why Father had hired Henry in the first place. Maybe Father hadn't really wanted to give up his sermons at all. But who would preach on Sundays now?

"How nice," exclaimed Louise as Alice set the tray on the white wicker table between the two women. "Alice, you're just too good to us. Sit down and take a break before you completely wear yourself out."

Aunt Ethel reached for a glass and smiled. "Daniel and I shared many a glass of lemonade out here over the years. It's hard to believe that only last week we were sitting here reminiscing about our childhoods. We discovered that even though he was much older and already out of the house by the time I came along, we'd actually had some very similar experiences." She sighed. "I'll miss those little chats with him."

Louise looked out over the still blooming climbing tea roses. "Well, it's certainly a beautiful place for visiting with family and friends." She smiled. "I'd almost forgotten how much I love this old porch and having a real yard to look out on."

Wendell jumped into her lap as Alice settled herself into the porch swing and looked out over the lawn now in need of mowing. "Yes, even though the grounds have been a bit neglected these past few years, the old flowers and shrubs still look pretty good." As she stroked the cat, she leaned back and listened to the gentle rhythmic squeaking of the swing as she moved back and forth. It had always been such a comforting sound.

"These are good," said Louise as she reached for her second cookie. "Did you bake them, Alice?"

"No, Patsy Ley brought them by."

"That's Pastor Ley's wife," said Aunt Ethel. "Have you met her yet?"

Louise shook her head no. "I barely remember Pastor Ley. Wasn't he a rather soft-spoken fellow?"

Aunt Ethel laughed. "That's one way of putting it."

"Have you thought about who's going to take over the Sunday sermons?" asked Alice. Aunt Ethel was on the church board, along with Alice and several other church members. Naturally, she was usually full of ideas for how things should be run at Grace Chapel.

"Well, now, that is a bit of a sticky problem. *Tsk-tsk,* the good Lord knows that Pastor Ley can't preach to save his soul."

Louise chuckled. "Then why on earth is he a pastor?"

"He's a good man," Alice explained. "Whenever a parishioner is in need, Pastor Ley is the first one to lend a hand or an ear or whatever. He has a real servant's heart."

"And absolutely no skills in public speaking. *Tsk-tsk,* he could profit from a lesson or two from my Lloyd."

Louise's brows rose slightly. "*Your* Lloyd, Aunt Ethel?"

Aunt Ethel waved her hand. "Oh, did I forget to mention that the mayor and I have been dating lately?"

Louise shook her head. "Going after younger men now?"

"Pish-posh, Louise, he's not that much younger." Aunt Ethel patted her stiffly sprayed hair. "Besides, haven't you heard that age is just a number?" She glanced at Alice. "Isn't that what you're always saying, dear?"

Alice shrugged. "Today I'm feeling like I'm pushing about a hundred."

"You should go take a nap, dear," suggested Louise. "You do seem tired, and I'm sure you've been through a lot today."

"Oh, I'm fine—"

"Now, Alice, I'm not your older sister for nothing. Listen to me. You need to go have a little rest. Then you can freshen up after your cleaning campaign on the kitchen. Really, I insist. Ethel and I are perfectly capable of handling things down here."

Alice slowly stood. "Okay, I suppose I could at least shower and change."

"Yes." Louise nodded firmly. "You'll feel much better if you do."

Alice obediently went to her room, feeling very much like a dismissed child, but she was unable to fall asleep. She'd never been much of a napper. Instead she took a cool shower and, after standing for a long time before the embarrassingly sparse selection of clothes in her closet, she finally selected a lightweight cotton dress. Father had always liked it, saying its shade of periwinkle looked well on her. She didn't normally wear dresses, other than to church, but decided that perhaps she should make a special effort for the first evening with her two sisters. Oh, if only Father could be here too.

She sat down in her easy chair by the window and picked up her old Bible. The cover had once been white but was now aged to a mellow creamy color. She wanted to read for a bit, to experience a little solace and comfort, but for some reason she just held the soft leather book in her lap. She remembered the day her father had given her that Bible, just shortly after Mother had died. He had presented both Louise and Alice with new Bibles then, along with a tender speech about how they were the "women of the house now." She had felt as if she'd aged by a decade during that brief period of time, as if her childhood had been laid aside from that day on. She and Louise had done their best to keep their household running smoothly. It wasn't long before they became like a pair of "mothers" to their new sister Jane. That's what women in the church liked to call the Howard girls, "the two little mothers."

"Alice!" yelled a familiar female voice from downstairs.

Alice hurried to the landing. "Jane?" she called back.

"Yes! I'm here, at last. You coming down?"

The next thing Alice knew, she and her sisters were hugging and talking at once.

"I'm so glad you're here!" exclaimed Alice as she stepped back to get a better look at her younger sister. Jane looked wan and tired with dark circles beneath her normally sparkling blue eyes. She also looked as if she'd lost weight.

"How was your flight?" asked Louise.

"Long and boring." Jane pushed a silver and turquoise bracelet up her thin wrist and sighed.

"Boring's better than being tossed around in turbulence," quipped Aunt Ethel. "It was so bumpy the last time I flew that a glass of juice went right in my lap."

"You look simply exhausted, Jane," said Louise. "Are you all right?"

"Just tired, I guess. I haven't been sleeping that well lately."

"Well, that's about to change," announced Alice. "It's much quieter here than in San Francisco. Just wait until you get into your old bed. You'll be sleeping like a log in no time."

Jane attempted a feeble smile. "Hope so."

"Are you hungry?" asked Aunt Ethel. "The church ladies have been stocking the refrigerator since yesterday. I'm sure that Alice has something yummy planned for dinner." She glanced at Alice expectantly.

Alice knew she was outflanked. She invited their aunt to join them for another meal.

"Oh, if it's no trouble. I'd love to stay." Aunt Ethel took

Jane by the arm now. "And now I can tell Jane all about Acorn Hill's latest—"

"I, for one, would like to hear about Jane's latest," interrupted Louise, taking Jane by the other arm. "Let's go put your bags in your room while Alice starts getting things out for dinner." She glanced at Alice. "Is that okay, dear? You've been such a trooper today. Perhaps Aunt Ethel would like to give you a hand—"

"Oh, I'm fine."

"I don't mind," offered Ethel. "How about if I set the table? Did you plan on eating in the formal dining room tonight?"

Alice really would have preferred the coziness of the kitchen, not to mention the company of her two sisters without any more "auntly" influence. Yet she knew Aunt Ethel was probably lonely, and they were, after all, family.

"The dining room is fine," said Alice as she removed a baking dish of ham and scalloped potatoes from the refrigerator and turned on the oven.

She poked around the refrigerator until she found a large stoneware bowl of coleslaw that Viola Reed had dropped by this afternoon. Viola wasn't a chapel member, but a good-hearted woman who ran the local bookstore. Alice paused to look out the kitchen window in time to see the sky growing pink—the same conch-shell color her skin had turned at the beach a few months ago when she and Father had taken an unexpected excursion one weekend. It had been a sunny June Saturday, and Father had suddenly set down his coffee cup and said, "I'd love to see the ocean today." Although Alice had already made arrangements with Vera, she hadn't minded canceling them. Then she drove them the four hours to the beach. It was a lovely day, and Father was so happy to see the ocean that he removed his shoes and waded right in. Alice sighed with relief. Thank God she had taken the time to go. She looked back up at the colorful sky and wondered how it could really be that late in the day already. Then she remembered that despite the unseasonable heat, it *was* September and the sun was going down earlier and earlier these days. It would soon be autumn. How Father had loved that time of year. She shook her head. Oh, what would she do without him?

Chapter Four

*J*ane, do you still paint?" asked Aunt Ethel as Alice served the blackberry pie for dessert. "I remember how much you loved to paint and draw when you were in high school."

"Actually, I've made an attempt to pick it up again. Sort of a form of therapy, after the divorce, you know."

"Therapy?" repeated Aunt Ethel. "Does that mean that it's been an unhappy divorce?"

"What divorce isn't unhappy?" said Alice.

"Well, they hadn't been married *that* long," said Aunt Ethel as if a short-term relationship couldn't break your heart as completely as a long one.

"It was nine years," said Alice. "That's a pretty big chunk of a lifetime."

Jane tossed an appreciative glance toward Alice. "I thought so too. Sometimes I wonder how I made it last even that long. I guess I kept thinking things would get better with time."

"But they didn't?" Louise asked, setting down her cup with a clink and shaking her head sadly.

Aunt Ethel frowned. "Are you absolutely sure you did everything possible to work it out, Jane?"

Jane looked down at her plate without answering.

"Of course she did," said Alice soothingly. "We all know that Jane's not the type to give up easily on anything. Remember when she was determined to build that tree house out back? No one could stop her. We just need to keep in mind that some things just aren't meant to be."

"I really wanted it to work." Jane sighed. "I mean, why wouldn't I? I loved Justin, but he just became so— so impossible."

"Well, all men can be difficult from time to time," injected Aunt Ethel. "Even my dear Bob, God bless his soul, could make me madder than a wet hen occasionally."

"But this was different." Jane put down her fork and looked at them with a surprising intensity. "When my cooking career started to take off, Justin completely changed. It was really weird—almost like Jekyll and Hyde. He simply couldn't handle my success."

Louise nodded. "Jealousy. That can happen when a couple shares the same vocation. Goodness, I remember a few times when Eliot resented me, like the first time I was invited to be a judge for the university's annual music competition. Why, it was such an honor for me! But poor Eliot felt he should've been asked. His nose was out of joint for a week. But then these little disputes have ways of sorting themselves out over time."

"Maybe for you, Louise," said Jane. "It's not always that easy for everyone."

"Oh, I don't know," said Aunt Ethel. "I tend to agree with Louise. I think young people are much too quick to give up on things these days. Why, I remember back when—"

"Excuse me," interrupted Jane. "I am very tired from my trip. I hope you don't mind if I turn in early tonight."

"Of course not," said Alice. "You look like you're due for some rest. Sleep as late as you like. Just take it easy."

After Jane left, Alice excused herself and began picking up the dinner dishes while Louise and Aunt Ethel continued discussing how the younger generation dealt with their problems nowadays.

Finally, when the kitchen was clean, Alice excused herself too. "It's been a long day," she said to the two older women now seated comfortably in the living room, still catching up on Acorn Hill's latest, although it looked like Louise was quickly wearying of her aunt's nearly nonstop chatter.

"Yes, dear," said Louise. "I won't be far behind you. I still believe in the 'early to bed, early to rise' adage—even more so the older I get."

Alice could see a ribbon of light under Jane's bedroom

door as she walked down the hallway. Hesitating for a moment, she decided to tap.

"Yes?"

"I just wanted to say good night, Jane."

The door opened slightly and Jane's pale face peered out. "Good night, Alice."

"I hope you won't let anything Louise or Aunt Ethel said tonight get to you."

Jane smiled ever so slightly and opened the door wider. "Want to come in?"

"Sure, if you're not going to bed right now."

"I just used that as an excuse to vacate. I didn't want to say anything I'd regret."

Alice smiled now. "Yes, I know the feeling. I don't really think that Louise means to sound so bossy, but I suppose Aunt Ethel gets her going."

"All that talk about not trying hard enough with Justin really hurts." Jane flopped down on her bed and leaned back against the aqua blue chenille pillows that Alice had made for her nearly four decades ago. Alice had spent most of a summer day measuring, cutting, and sewing the covers from an old bedspread that had once belonged to their mother.

Alice sat down in the rocking chair next to the bed and nodded. "She shouldn't have said that, Jane. I'm sure you gave it all you had."

"I really did. I begged him to go to counseling. He wouldn't. I went, but it didn't change things. You see, Alice, he walked out on me."

Jane quickly brushed away the tear that had slipped down her cheek. "I never planned on telling the family all the details of my failed marriage, Alice. I'm not even sure why. Maybe I was just embarrassed. Justin was so jealous of me that he actually began sabotaging my career. At first I thought I was imagining it, and then it became plain that he was trying to ruin me, not to mention my reputation. It took several good friends confronting me with the truth before I even really accepted it. Justin has what you'd call a passive-aggressive personality."

Alice nodded. "Seems pretty easygoing, but it's just a cover-up."

"A cover-up that they use to control you. They act like they don't care about a situation, then when you're not expecting it they pull the rug out from under you."

Alice shook her head. "I'm so sorry, Jane. I wish that you had called me and talked about this. I mean if it would've helped."

"I almost called you a number of times, Alice. But I knew you'd have to tell Father. I didn't want to disappoint him. I so badly wanted to be the grownup and handle my own problems. You know how I've always felt like the baby in this family. As if no matter what I did I would never be quite equal to the grownups." She shook her head. "Good grief, here I am a fifty-year-old woman and I still feel like a complete child sometimes."

Alice smiled. "That's not so bad. Do you remember how Jesus said we should all become like children?"

Jane seemed to consider this. "Well, I suppose I've got a head start on that one."

"I have a feeling we could all learn a lot from you."

Jane sighed. "I don't see how."

"Perhaps that's the beauty in it."

Jane got up from the bed and put her arms around Alice. "I love you, Alice. You've always been so kind and understanding. You make me really glad to be home again."

"And I'm so glad that you're here," said Alice. She glanced around the room. "As I told Louise, I'm sorry I couldn't clean up in here more—"

"Oh, Alice!" Jane shook her head. "No apologies. You made yourself way too much of a slave for us already. I insist that I help out in the kitchen while I'm here—if you don't mind, that is."

"Mind? Are you kidding? You know what kind of a cook I am. But I don't want you feeling like you have to—"

"That's not it. I *want* to. I feel completely lost without

a kitchen floor under my feet. I promise that I'll try not to take over."

Alice waved her hand. "Feel free to take over."

Jane smiled. "So, tell me, how's your job going?"

Alice felt mildly surprised. Father was the only one in the family who had ever inquired about her work before, but then Jane had always been a lot like Father. "It's been going pretty well. I'm head nurse on my shift now and I really like my crew. I can't imagine what I'd do without my job. Naturally, I felt caught off guard yesterday, with the phone call about Father and all. I guess I sort of lost it emotionally. But my administrator was so sweet about it. He insisted I take two weeks off."

"That's nice."

"I guess so, although I'm not sure what I'll do to stay busy for that long. But then you and Louise are here, and I'm sure we've got a lot of catching up to do."

"That's right."

"Well, you really do look tired, Jane. I think I should let you get some rest."

"Thanks for coming in to talk."

"Thanks for letting me."

Alice slipped back out into the hallway, then up the stairs to her own room on the third floor. Alice had opted for a room there when she'd moved back home. For one thing, it had a perfect view of the chapel, but also it made her feel more independent to have the whole floor to herself.

She quietly closed the door behind her and considered her conversation with Jane. It was reassuring to hear her sister's explanation for not coming to visit more often. And now that she thought about it, it did make perfect sense. Still she wondered why Jane hadn't spoken more of their father or even his death. Perhaps Jane simply accepted that he was old and it was his time to go. The pain of losing Father still felt fresh to Alice. But then she reminded herself for the umpteenth time that death was simply a natural part of life. Everyone had to die at some point in time—after all, it was the only way they could begin their eternal lives.

Alice turned on the light on her bureau and looked around her cheerful room. It seemed to welcome her. Until yesterday, she had almost forgotten how the Howard girls' original bedrooms on the second floor were still trapped in some kind of a time warp. Louise's room, with its pink ruffled canopy bed, was straight out of the fifties, whereas Jane's looked like a slice of the sixties with its mod style of paisley and daisies and wild neon colors. Since neither sister had ever lived at home after college, it was only natural that their rooms would remain the same. Father, always busy with chapel responsibilities, had certainly seen no reason to change anything. Alice felt a bit guilty that she hadn't done anything herself. But then her life, like Father's, was usually busy too. She hoped that her sisters wouldn't mind. Perhaps they'd even enjoy taking the trip down memory lane again.

When Alice had decided to switch rooms, she'd also taken the time to create a space that made her feel comfortable. She had painted the walls a nice buttery yellow, inspired by the old patchwork quilt she'd found in a trunk in the attic. It had been in perfect condition. Father had said it had been made by Alice's maternal grandmother as a wedding gift for him and his wife nearly seventy years ago, but he assured Alice that she was more than welcome to it, that the colors had always been a bit too feminine for his taste. Alice loved the quilt and felt that it provided a connection to her mother and the Berry side of the family, and she thought the soft pastel hues of yellow, green, and violet were perfectly lovely. She'd even braided a cotton area rug with colors that matched the quilt. It had taken the better part of one winter to complete it. Father had called it her rainbow project since the arcs of yellow, lavender and green really did resemble a rainbow.

"I love you, Father," she whispered quietly. "If you can hear me, just know that I really do love you. I should've told you that more often than I did. I hope you knew. And I know that you loved me. I hope you're happy in heaven. But I sure do miss you."

Chapter Five

I'm guessing that's about the biggest funeral service this town has ever seen," commented Fred Humbert as he helped himself to another piece of Martha Bevins's applesauce cake, the recipe that had won her a blue ribbon at the county fair nearly twenty years ago.

"I really appreciated what you said about Father, Fred." Alice poured another pitcher of fruit punch into the nearly empty bowl. "I'm sure Father would've liked it too."

"Just the plain and simple truth," said Fred.

"That's right," agreed his wife Vera. "Daniel Howard had a big hand in making this town what it is today. There's no disputing that."

"You've got that right," said Lloyd Tynan as he glanced around the crowded chapel basement. "And you've got all these good people to attest to the fact." He lowered his voice a bit. "I just hope the fire marshal's not doing a head count right now. We'd be shut down in an instant."

"Fortunately quite a few people have already left," said

Aunt Ethel. "And with luck the rest will clear out before we run completely out of food."

"Oh, Aunt Ethel," scolded Louise.

Lloyd leaned over toward Louise. "That piece you played at the end of the service was magnificent, Louise."

Louise straightened her pearls and smiled. "Why, thank you, Lloyd."

Aunt Ethel bristled slightly. "Did you know that Louise teaches music in Philadelphia, Lloyd?" She glanced at her eldest niece. "I expect you'll need to be getting back to your students before too long."

Louise glanced around the warm and noisy room and smiled. The Gardner twins were playing a game of tag around the tables, and old Mrs. Avery was loudly retelling an incident that had occurred at a church picnic nearly fifty years ago. "Goodness me," Louise sighed. "I've hardly even thought about going back to the city. It's just so good to be back home again. Who knows, maybe I'll decide to stick around."

Aunt Ethel blinked. "Really?"

"Are you serious?" asked Alice hopefully. "You'd think about moving back here?"

Louise nodded. "Actually, I've been thinking about it for some time now . . . ever since Eliot passed on. With Cynthia living away from home now . . . well, sometimes I feel like a ship without an anchor."

"Cynthia?" asked Lloyd. "Is that your daughter?"

"Yes, my only child. Poor Cynthia couldn't make the funeral. She flew on business to Frankfurt, Germany, the morning Father died and just couldn't come right back home. I'm sure my father would understand perfectly."

Lloyd nodded. "I'm sure he would, Louise. So, tell me, are you really considering moving back here?"

Louise sighed. "There's no real reason for me to stay in Philadelphia."

Aunt Ethel seemed concerned. "But really, Louise, wouldn't you find Acorn Hill to be a little . . . well, small potatoes . . . compared to an important bustling place like Philadelphia?"

Louise smiled. "Sometimes small potatoes are the tastiest."

"What's this about potatoes?" asked Jane as she joined them.

Alice laughed. "Actually it was a metaphor. Louise is considering moving back home to Acorn Hill."

Jane turned to her oldest sister. "Really?"

"Oh, I haven't made up my mind yet. I must admit that I am certainly enjoying the slower pace of a small town. The people seem so friendly, and, well, it just feels like home to me."

"That's because it is," said Alice. "Father would be so pleased to hear you say that."

"I think he'd be pleased with the way that you organized this memorial service today, Alice," said Jane. "It was so touching the way everyone got up and shared a personal memory about him."

"I can't take all the credit," said Alice. "It was something Pastor Ley and I worked out together."

"Anyway, it was just perfect," said Louise. "It felt like he was right here among us."

"I think he was," said Jane in a quiet voice.

"Well, Daniel Howard can be proud," said Lloyd with a wide grin. "Why, just look at how fine his three daughters turned out." He glanced over to Ethel and added, "And his sister's not half bad either."

They all laughed at this. Alice tried to imagine her father smiling down upon his family. She hoped he was proud of his daughters. But it troubled her that he hadn't been able to spend some time with them all before his final departure. If only her sisters had been able to come more often.

As the crowd slowly dwindled, Alice slipped away from the reception and got into her little blue Toyota and drove back toward the cemetery. She wasn't even sure why, since they'd already paid their last respects at the gravesite earlier today. But with so many people present, Alice had felt lost in the crowd. She wanted a quiet moment on her own now.

The grave was still awash in a sea of colorful flowers.

Despite the family's request that donations be sent to the chapel's Helping Hands program in lieu of floral arrangements, they had still received a truckload of blooms. "It's just the town's own way of paying its respects and saying good-bye," Fred Humbert had observed.

Alice stood and looked at the new grave in front of the family headstone. Soon "Daniel Joseph Howard" would be neatly etched into the granite right next to her mother's name, "Madeleine Louise Berry Howard," along with "Together at last." Alice smiled to herself when she tried to imagine the reunion that her two parents must have enjoyed in heaven that morning several days ago.

"Are you happy, Father?" she spoke the words aloud, then glanced over her shoulder as if she expected someone to be listening. "You're with Mother now. That must be nice." She sighed and glanced at her watch. She had better get home before her sisters grew concerned about her absence.

Louise and Jane were walking from the chapel to the house when Alice parked her car in the driveway. They didn't ask where she had been, but chattered about the events of the day, how well it had all gone, and Aunt Ethel's little jealousy attack when Lloyd had complimented Louise.

"As if I'd really be interested," said Louise in what Jane used to jokingly call her "highbrow" tone. Not that Louise had ever been a snob, but she did know how to get the upper hand when necessary.

"Oh, come on, Louie," teased Jane as she sat down in the porch swing and scooped Wendell into her lap. "You could do worse than old Lloyd."

Alice sat down in a wicker rocker without speaking.

"What's wrong, Alice?" asked Louise after a bit.

Alice shrugged. "Guess I'm feeling sad."

Jane nodded. "Missing Father?"

"I guess so."

"Well, it's bound to be harder on you, Alice," said Louise gently. "You lived here with him for years. It's only natural that you'd miss him."

Alice swallowed against the lump in her throat.

"So what's to become of the old place?" asked Jane.

"The old place?" Alice peered at Jane.

"You know," Jane waved her arms. "The old family home."

"The house has really gone downhill," added Louise. "Needs painting and I'm guessing a new roof. What's it been—about forty years since it was last done? I'm surprised it's even holding up."

"I had offered to help pay for it," said Alice weakly. "But you know Father, he just wouldn't hear of it." She stood. "I think I'll go change into something more comfortable." She could hear her two sisters still chatting pleasantly as she went inside the house. It was nice to see that they were getting along better today. Perhaps it was Alice's turn to be "odd man out."

As she changed into jeans and a chambray shirt, she wondered why she hadn't told her sisters the news about their father's intentions for the family home yet. What was she waiting for anyway? Even though she'd made Aunt Ethel promise to keep quiet, you just couldn't count on that woman to remain silent for very long, especially with important family matters like this. In fact, Aunt Ethel had already nagged her about it twice. Alice decided that she'd better explain the whole business at dinner tonight.

Alice walked downstairs to find the porch vacant and the house quiet. Perhaps her sisters were resting in their rooms now. She walked around and looked at the familiar scenes that had been a part of her life for so many years. As she ran her hand over the oak banister, it occurred to her that her reason for remaining quiet about the house was most likely due to fear. She was afraid that Jane and Louise might want to sell the old place. And who could blame them really? Jane could probably invest her share into the restaurant business. And perhaps it would help Louise to relocate closer to her daughter. But then where would that put Alice? Of course, she knew she could always find another place to live, but it would never be home—not like this.

She decided to walk into town and pick up a pint of half-and-half. Jane had mentioned that she liked to have real cream in her coffee in the mornings. Besides it was a good excuse to get some exercise. Normally she walked with Vera three mornings a week, but that had been put on hold during the past few hectic days. She missed her good friend's company. Even though Alice was ten years older than Vera, the two had bonded right from the start. Alice still remembered the day Fred first introduced his fiancé to Alice and how much she liked the sensible young woman. When Alice hosted a church bridal shower for Vera, their friendship was sealed.

Alice decided to stop by the Coffee Shop and say hello to Hope, whom she had spied at the service earlier today. She'd had on her waitress uniform, and Alice had guessed she'd taken time off in order to come. Alice had wanted to speak to her then, but never got the chance.

The Coffee Shop was quiet, not unusual for this time of afternoon. The bell on the door had barely rung before Hope popped out from the kitchen. "Hi, Alice," she said as she set down a bag of sugar. "What're you up to?"

"Just taking a walk to get out of the house."

Hope nodded. "Yeah, all that family time can be trying sometimes."

Alice smiled and sat down on a stool by the counter. "Do you have any iced tea?"

"You bet."

"Hello, Alice," called the only other customer, Craig Tracy, seated in a booth by the window. Alice barely knew him but had heard her father mention his name from time to time. Most folks still considered Craig a "newcomer," meaning he hadn't been born and raised in Acorn Hill. As a result most weren't too sure about him yet, although Fred Humbert had recently spoken highly of him. Craig owned a small florist business called Wild Things, and judging by the number of arrangements on her father's grave, he'd been fairly busy this past week.

"How're you doing, Craig?"

"All right. Sorry to hear about your dad. He was a great old man."

"Did you know him well?"

"Yes. He and I used to chat on a regular basis."

Hope set a tall glass of iced tea in front of Alice. "Yeah, Craig and Daniel used to get pretty rambunctious in here sometimes, especially when they were talking about religion."

"Just enthusiastic," Craig corrected her. "Daniel had some impressive beliefs, and I didn't mind challenging him when I could."

Hope laughed. "Not that you could rattle him. Despite his age Daniel was sharp, and there's no denying he enjoyed a good debate."

Alice smiled. "That's the truth."

"That was a nice service today," said Hope as she filled up a sugar container. "I especially liked what you had to say about your dad."

Alice tried to remember her exact words, but it was a little blurry. She hadn't written down her thoughts, but had simply spoken from her heart.

"The part about how your dad got you out of school and drove you to the mountains after your dog died made me cry," continued Hope.

"That was a special day."

Alice visited with the two of them for a bit longer before she headed on over to the store to buy the half-and-half and a couple of plump red tomatoes that were too tempting to pass up. Thankfully, the weather had cooled a bit today. Maybe autumn was around the corner after all. As she crossed Hill Street she sighed at the comforting familiarity of the buildings. So little had changed during the course of her lifetime.

Yet, just as she stepped from the street onto the curb, it hit her that something was very different. She wondered what it was as she continued walking toward home, and then finally decided it was simply that Father would no longer be walking down these sidewalks. That fact alone made the town seem changed somehow. As she strolled past the chapel and turned up the walk to her own house, she decided that the loss of her father would most definitely alter her world. Although this needn't be a negative thing. God was still in control of her life. Father had always been a man to welcome change. Perhaps it was time for her to follow his example and accept that she was stepping into a whole new era. Who knew what tomorrow might bring?

Chapter Six

*A*ll three women appeared to be waiting for Alice's entrance when she stepped into the kitchen. She could tell by their troubled expressions that something was wrong. She set her small bag on the counter and asked if there was a problem.

Louise cleared her throat and then announced, "Aunt Ethel has just informed us that Father left the family home to the three of us."

Aunt Ethel smiled somewhat nervously. It was clear that she was going nowhere just now, when she had a front row seat for what might prove an interesting show.

Alice took in a deep breath. "Aunt Ethel, I told you that I planned to tell them. Why couldn't you just wait until—"

"Well, it just slipped out, Alice," her aunt explained quickly. "I simply mentioned to Jane that Lloyd was telling me about a new realtor in the area who'd probably be interested in listing it—"

"Why didn't you tell us, Alice?" asked Jane. "Were you worried that we'd want to sell it?"

"Not really, I just—"

"Is there anything else we need to know?" asked Louise.

"No, of course—"

Aunt Ethel adjusted her pink cardigan sweater. "You know, I've read that dividing up a family's wealth can create some nasty feuds." She nodded her head so vigorously that both sets of chins bobbed at once.

"Father didn't have any wealth," said Alice in a firmer than usual voice. "He stopped taking a salary ages ago and his retirement pension was barely enough to pay for the utilities and taxes, let alone food. He had absolutely no savings whatsoever. During his final years he decided that it was wrong for him to store up riches as long as there were people going hungry in the world."

"So there's not a lawyer or a will?" asked Louise with slightly raised brows.

"No, Louise, Father asked me to handle it for him."

"Then why didn't you tell us—"

"Jane, Louise," Alice tried to keep her voice level. "It's not as if I was trying to hide something from you. I was just waiting for—"

"No one is accusing you of hiding anything, Alice," said Louise. "But it would have made things clearer if Father had written down his wishes. Are you absolutely certain that he didn't?"

"He told me what his wishes were—"

"But have you checked in his study, Alice, or in his desk or journal?"

Alice shrugged. "Feel free to look around." Suddenly she felt like sobbing, but instead turned around and slowly filled the old copper teakettle with cold water, then set it on the stove and clicked on the flame. She could hear her aunt talking about things like Grandmother Howard's oak dresser and her mother's sterling silver coffee set, but it wasn't long before the sentence fragments simply floated over her like a stream of white noise. She stood and silently watched the blue flame of the stove, waiting for the teakettle to whistle and break this spell.

The three other women were in her father's study where Alice suspected they were now going through his personal papers. *Fine*, she thought as she carefully poured the steaming water into the rosebud covered porcelain teapot, *let them*. For all she cared they could discover some hidden document stating that every single piece of their family's possessions was meant to go to—to China! That would be perfectly fine with her. What did it really matter anyway?

She took her favorite cup and saucer, the one with dainty little violets, and set them on a tray with the teapot, then quietly tiptoed up to her room before she closed her door. She decided she wasn't really hungry, and Louise and Jane could easily fix their own dinner from all the leftovers tonight. She was bone tired right now, and who knew what tomorrow would bring? She suspected that she was overreacting. Perhaps they were all overreacting. After all, they had just lost their father, and there were numerous matters to be sorted out. Certainly it all could wait until morning.

After a night of fitful sleep, Alice got up before the sun. She pulled on her gray hooded sweatshirt, comfortable jeans and walking shoes, then slipped out of the house and started along the route that she and Vera usually took. She hoped that the exercise might help to clarify her thoughts. Then, almost done but still feeling a bit frustrated, she decided to stop by her old walking buddy's house. Since it was Saturday, she suspected that Vera might not be up yet, but Alice hoped that she'd forgive this early intrusion. She knocked on the door, reassuring herself that Fred was probably awake.

"Alice." Fred looked slightly surprised when he opened the door wide. "Come on in, I just put on a pot of coffee." Then he smiled. "Of course, I forgot. You don't drink coffee, do you?"

"Perhaps it's time for a change," she said decisively as she stepped in the door with her chin held firmly.

His brows rose slightly. "Oh boy, something must really be wrong."

"Who's that?" called Vera.

"Alice is here, honey," answered Fred.

"Oh dear." Vera appeared in the kitchen wearing sponge rollers and a pink bathrobe. "Were we supposed to walk this morning?"

Alice shook her head. "No, I'm sorry to wake you up so early, Vera, but I really need to talk."

Vera smiled. "Oh, good. I thought maybe I'd forgotten."

Fred set three mugs of coffee on the kitchen table. "You take anything in yours, Alice?"

"Alice doesn't drink coffee, Fred."

"I do now," said Alice.

"Good grief," exclaimed Vera. "What on earth's the matter, Alice?"

Alice poured out her story to her two good friends. Somehow hearing the words out loud made it all seem a little less disturbing. Before long the three of them were actually laughing at the idea of Louise scouring through Daniel's study in search of some secret papers or clandestine will.

"Sounds like Louise is a bit out of touch," said Vera.

"Well, I'm sure it seems odd to her that Father didn't have a lawyer or do something more official," Alice defended.

"Did she know her father very well?" asked Fred.

Alice shook her head. "I'm not really sure."

"So what do you think they'll want to do with the house

now?" he asked. "Surely they've noticed that it's in need of some serious repairs."

Alice shrugged. "I don't know. I guess I'd hoped that we could keep it somehow, but I suppose that's not the most practical idea."

"It's possible that they might want to sell it," said Vera. "In some ways it seems the sensible thing to do."

"Won't be easy to sell a big place like that." Fred refilled his coffee cup. "Don't know anyone in town needing that much room these days."

"Besides that, it'll probably cost a fortune to repair it," added Vera. "Maybe you'd be better off just getting rid of it altogether, Alice. You could always buy a smaller house."

"Maybe."

Fred glanced at the clock above the table. "Guess I'd better head down to the store. I've got an early shipment of rakes and brooms coming this morning."

"Thanks for listening," said Alice. "And for the coffee."

"Looks like you're not going to be much of a coffee drinker," said Vera as she looked at Alice's still nearly full cup.

Alice sighed.

"The kettle's hot. How about some tea?"

"That'd be nice."

"Too bad there's not some way to make money with the old house, some kind of cottage industry or antique shop or something. My sister Wanda up in Vermont is thinking about turning her house into a tearoom to help her make ends meet." Vera set a cup of golden tea in front of Alice. "Although I doubt there's much money in that sort of thing."

"You know, Vera, there is something I've fantasized about for years."

Vera leaned forward with interest. "What? Is it a man?"

Alice laughed. "Well, no, although I've probably fantasized about that too. But sometimes I used to dream about turning the house into a bed and breakfast. Of course, I never mentioned this idea to Father. I couldn't imagine he'd go for something like that. But now I wonder . . ."

"I don't know." Vera frowned. "Acorn Hill isn't exactly your tourist type of town."

"But it's such a sweet little place, old-fashioned and quaint. Don't you think city people would find it charming?"

"If they could even find it at all."

"And it could help the local businesses. More visitors means more commerce."

"Maybe, but don't forget there are plenty of folks in this town who like things just fine the way they are."

"I know." Alice sipped her tea and daydreamed a bit more, imagining the interesting sorts of people she might possibly meet in her bed and breakfast. "But sometimes change is good, Vera."

"What about your sisters and their part interest in the house? I wonder what they would think of this idea?"

Alice sighed. "Good question. For all I know they may be meeting with a realtor right now."

"Not without your permission, they'd better not."

Alice forced a smile. "I'm sure that they wouldn't do that."

"Good grief, you'd think those two would be more appreciative. After all you've done over the years, taking care of your father the way you have. Pastor Daniel was their dad too."

Alice shook her head. "To be honest, there's another thing that's been nagging me lately, Vera. It seems sort of silly, but I keep thinking about how Father wanted to see all three of us together again. But Jane and Louise were always too busy. I realize they had their own lives and responsibilities and all, but it just bothers me."

Vera patted her hand. "Don't you think Pastor Daniel is looking down right now? Don't you think he can see his three daughters together?"

Alice blinked as she set down her cup. "Goodness, that doesn't make me feel much better . . . especially when I think of how frustrated all three of us have been with each other. Poor Father."

"I have a feeling Pastor Daniel can handle it now." Vera gave her a gentle smile. "Sometimes these family relationships just take a little time and patience to work out. It's no secret that you three are just as different as can be. Only yesterday at the service I heard Ellen Moore comment on how she couldn't believe you three were actually related, let alone flesh and blood sisters."

"It is rather interesting, isn't it?"

"Well, for some reason your father believed that leaving the house to the three of you would bring you together. Pastor Daniel was no fool, Alice. I expect it's just a matter of time before you work this thing out."

"I hope you're right."

"Knowing you, I don't know how I could be wrong. You have a gift when it comes to working things out."

"I'm not so sure anymore, Vera. I was pretty fed up last night."

"Did you tell your sisters how you felt?"

Alice looked down at her nearly empty cup but said nothing.

"Just as I thought."

"I suppose I should get back now, Vera. They might be worried."

"Might do them some good if they were worried. They should appreciate you a little more."

"I'm sure they do, Vera." Alice stood. "If I said anything wrong about my sisters, I hope you'll forgive me and just take it with a grain of salt. You know that I love them."

"I know, I know. Sometimes it's good to vent these things, and your conversation is always safe with me. But, really, Alice, I don't like to think of them taking advantage of you."

"They're my sisters, Vera. And despite everything, I know that they love me too. Besides that, remember what Jesus said: to be great in God's kingdom, you must become a servant."

"Servant maybe. But not a doormat."

Alice smiled as she reached for the back door. "Thanks, Vera, for the tea and sympathy."

"Anytime. Well, as long as it's not a school day." Vera patted her sponge rollers and laughed. "Good grief, I completely forgot how I look. By the way, you ready to start walking again? I think I've put five extra pounds onto these hips since we stopped."

"I'm with you. How about if we get back on our old schedule starting on Monday."

Chapter Seven

*J*ane was rinsing out a bowl in the kitchen sink when Alice slipped in the back door.

"Something smells good," said Alice in a friendly voice.

Jane turned quickly. "Oh, Alice! There you are. I was so worried." She dried off her hands on a towel and approached her sister. "I'm sorry about our stupidity last night."

"Well, I'll admit I was a little irked."

"Irked? You should've told us both to take a hike. Here you've been taking such good care of everyone." She shook her head. "I'm so sorry."

Alice reached out her arms and hugged her little sister. "Oh, Jane, you know I couldn't stay mad at you for very long."

"How about me?" Louise stepped into the kitchen with a guilty expression. Her normally perfectly coiffed hair was tussled from sleep, and she wore a pale blue dressing gown. "I'm sorry, Alice."

Alice hugged Louise too. "I think maybe we were all just feeling a little edgy yesterday," she said. "It had been such a demanding day with the funeral and all. Let's just chalk it up to stress."

"*And* Aunt Ethel," added Louise.

Alice smiled. "I don't think any of us were really at our best."

"I have a peace offering in the oven." Jane bent down to peek inside. "Cinnamon rolls and they're almost done."

"Oh, I simply adore your cinnamon rolls, Jane," said Louise. "I know you sent me your recipe, but honestly, no matter how hard I try, they never turn out as good as yours."

Jane took a mock bow. "That's why I get paid to do this."

Soon they were all seated around the kitchen table pulling apart the sweet and sticky confections.

"These are magnificent," said Alice. "Too bad you can't open up a restaurant in Acorn Hill, Jane."

Jane leaned back in the wooden chair and got a faraway look in her eye. "Who says I can't?"

Louise sat up straighter and adjusted her dressing gown. "What do you mean, Jane?"

"Oh, I don't know exactly. I guess I'm just thinking out loud. This past year has been so hard on me. Sometimes I want to just run away and leave everything behind. I used to love the city—the art, the culture, the music, even the fog, but more and more it's just a big lonely place that's too full of painful memories. I'm surprised to admit that Acorn Hill feels like a breath of fresh air to me right now."

"Really?" Alice could feel her heart starting to pound with anticipation. "Would you seriously consider relocating here?"

Jane nodded. "The truth is I stayed awake until three this morning thinking about it, trying to figure out if it's even plausible."

"What did you come up with?" asked Louise.

Jane sighed. "I'm not sure. I'd love to be able to start up a little restaurant or something small right here in Acorn Hill, but I'm just not sure I'm up for that kind of undertaking just yet."

"It would take quite a bit of effort to start up a restaurant," agreed Alice. She paused for a moment, carefully considering her next words. Was she rushing things? Or was she simply taking the next step? She studied her sisters' faces and thought how wonderful it was for the three of them to be together like this. So she continued. "What if there was some other option? Some enterprise that could possibly be a family business."

"Like what?" Jane set down her coffee mug and leaned forward with interest.

"Yes," said Louise eagerly. "What exactly do you have in mind?"

Alice felt a rush of hope. Could it be possible that

Father's last wishes might actually come true after all? "Well, I got to thinking this morning," she began in a quiet but intense voice. "Actually, Vera and I were talking about something . . ."

"What is it?" Jane's blue eyes grew brighter.

"Well, I know it might sound crazy."

"Come on," urged Louise. "Out with it."

"Okay. As you may have guessed, I've been hoping we could avoid selling the family home. I know that it's in need of repair. So Vera and I were talking about the whole thing . . . and suddenly I remembered this old dream of mine." Alice looked around the spacious but cluttered and fairly rundown kitchen, and then continued. "I think, with a little work, okay, maybe a lot of work, I think that this old house would make a lovely bed and breakfast."

"A bed and breakfast?" Louise seemed to chew on this.

"You know, an inn of sorts. A place where people could come to relax and unwind and—"

"Eat good food," added Jane with a twinkle in her eye. "Oh, Alice, who would you get to cook for you?"

"A renowned chef?" asked Alice hopefully.

Jane nodded. "I think so."

"Slow down, girls," warned Louise. "This would be an enormous undertaking."

"I know. I know." Alice sighed. "But wouldn't it be fun?"

"It doesn't hurt to kick the idea around a bit," said Jane.

"I guess not." Louise smiled. "To be honest, Eliot and I used to talk about buying an old house in the country and trying something like this. We stayed at this lovely place in Connecticut one summer, and the couple running it seemed to be having such a good time."

"There isn't anything like that around here," said Alice.

"We'd have to do some renovations on the house first," said Jane. "Especially this kitchen."

"It would be very expensive," said Louise.

"An investment," said Jane.

"I've got some money in my savings," offered Alice.

"I have money from my half of the sale of the house," said Jane. "It's not much, but I'm willing to—"

"It's a risky thing," said Louise, "pouring all your savings into this old place. What if the bed and breakfast didn't work out?"

"Well, we'd have a house that was more valuable than before," said Jane. "Even if we decided to sell it, we'd probably make some money in the end."

"I suppose," said Louise.

Alice considered this. She didn't like the idea of improving the house and being forced to sell. "Do you really think a bed and breakfast wouldn't work, Louise?"

Louise waved her hand. "No, I'm not suggesting that. Actually I just read an article about how they are more popular than ever on the East Coast. They even have a B and B association that publishes a directory."

"Okay, let's get back to the finances," said Jane. "Between Alice's savings and my money from the house—"

"Now, wait just a minute!" Louise stood up and held up her hands. "Don't you two go leaving me out of this whole thing. Remember I own one third of this house. I have a legitimate vote here."

They both turned and looked at Louise.

"Not that we're voting yet," said Louise with a smile. "I just don't want to be left out."

Jane raised one eyebrow. "And if we were voting, what would your vote be, Louise?"

"Well, do you think I could teach piano lessons here without upsetting the guests too much?"

"I don't see why not," said Jane. "Maybe we could use Father's den as a practice room."

Alice grinned. "Perhaps you could play for the guests occasionally."

"Do you really think they'd enjoy that?"

"Of course," exclaimed Alice. "What would be more lovely than enjoying one of Jane's delicious breakfasts while listening to a beautiful selection of classical piano played by one of Philadelphia's finest?"

Louise blinked. "Perhaps you should write that down, Alice. It sounds like something we could use in a promotional brochure."

"So, it sounds like you're on board, Louise," said Jane.

"I definitely think we should look into the possibilities," said Louise. "If we're really serious, that is."

Jane reached over and grabbed both of their hands. "So, what do we really think, girls? Are we all in this venture together?"

"I am," said Alice. "Even though it's risky, I feel it's worth it."

"So do I," said Jane. "I don't know any other two people that I'd rather partner with." She turned and looked at Louise. "Are you with us, big sister?"

Louise nodded with tears in her eyes. "We'll be like the three musketeers," she said happily. "All for one and one for all."

Alice felt her eyes filling too. Only now they were tears of pure joy. "Oh, Father would be so proud of us!"

"I'm sure that he is, Alice," said Louise. "He's probably up there clapping his hands right now."

Jane nodded. "And Mother too."

"May we bow our heads for a moment," suggested

Alice. They agreed and she led her sisters in a short but heartfelt prayer, dedicating their home and future bed and breakfast to God and to serving others.

"What shall we call it?" asked Jane.

"Well, a lot of folks in town refer to this as the Grace Chapel house, since we're right next to the chapel. What if we called it Grace Chapel Inn?"

"Grace Chapel Inn," repeated Louise. "That has a nice ring to it."

"I like it," agreed Jane.

Alice sighed as she reached down to give the snoozing Wendell a pat. She could hardly believe that she and her sisters had decided to change their home as well as the course of their lives over cinnamon rolls. She still wasn't sure how all the details would be worked out, and she knew there would be lots of decisions to make—from three very different women with three very differing sets of views. But she hoped that with God leading . . . they would find their way.

By mid-morning they had several well-developed to-do lists. And, to Alice's amazement, with all three women's financial contributions, it appeared that they might indeed be able to do a decent renovation of their home. As it turned out, Louise had managed to squirrel away quite a bit of money.

"Yes, at the time I thought that my poor Eliot might actually have turned over in his grave," Louise laughed, "or perhaps shaken his fist down from heaven. I cashed out most of our stocks a few years ago and put the money into my savings account."

"You're kidding!" Jane looked astounded.

"It's true. You see, I'd always been uncomfortable with the stock market. To me it was like purchasing a piece of air for a lot of money, but Eliot thought it was great fun and he was fairly successful. He was always investing in this or that. I had no idea of how much until after he'd passed away."

"So you must've got out before—"

"Before everything started going downhill."

"Lucky you," said Jane.

"I recently considered other sorts of investments, but I've never been quite sure what would be best. But I do like the idea of investing in real estate. I've always believed in concrete things like bricks and plaster, and feel much better about putting money into something I can see and touch."

"Like Grace Chapel Inn," said Alice.

"Exactly."

"*Yoo-hoo*," called an all too familiar voice. "Anyone home?"

"We're in the kitchen, Aunt Ethel," called Alice.

"Oh, good." Aunt Ethel clapped her hands. "It looks as if you've all made up. Now wouldn't Daniel be pleased."

Alice took in a deep breath.

"Yes, I think Father would be happy to see that we've all come to a good decision," said Jane.

"A decision?"

"Shall we tell her?" asked Louise in a conspirator's tone.

"I guess so," said Jane, although she sounded a bit unsure. "Maybe Alice should do the telling, since it was really her idea."

"Alice has an idea?" Aunt Ethel looked as if this were something unique.

Alice glanced at her sisters again, still not completely convinced that they had all agreed on this remarkable enterprise. They both nodded as if to encourage her. "Well, Aunt Ethel, we've decided to turn our house into an inn."

Aunt Ethel's eyes widened in horror. "*An inn?* What on earth for?"

"Because we think it would be fun," said Alice.

"*Fun?*" Aunt Ethel looked aghast.

"Yes," said Jane. "It'll be a bed and breakfast. I'll do the cooking. Louise will do an occasional bit of entertaining on the piano. Alice is great at organizing. Anyway, it's all falling neatly into place."

"Does this mean you and Louise plan to stay on in Acorn Hill for good?"

"For good or for bad," said Louise with a wry smile.

"For better or for worse," added Jane.

"*An inn?*" repeated Aunt Ethel as if she were still recovering from some sort of horrific shock.

"That's right." Alice held up a notepad. "We've already begun to plan and it seems that it all will work out."

"*Tsk-tsk*, that's only on paper," said Aunt Ethel.

"On paper is where we start," said Jane.

"So you're really not returning to San Francisco?" asked Aunt Ethel.

Jane shook her head in a firm "no."

"And you're not going back to Philadelphia, Louise?"

"Only to sell my house and take care of a few things."

"Oh my." Aunt Ethel sank into an empty chair and fanned herself with a napkin as if she were completely stunned or about to have a heart attack, although Alice knew from experience that it was only theatrics.

"Aren't you happy to have your other two nieces so close by?" asked Alice.

"Well, of course, dear. It's just that it's all something of a shock."

"We're still surprised too," said Louise. "But it feels right to me."

"We think that Father would be happy too," added Alice.

Now Aunt Ethel started to chuckle. "Well, this is something I will have to see with my own two eyes. The three Howard sisters all living and working together under one roof!"

Alice felt slightly defensive now, but at the same time knew that Aunt Ethel wasn't completely off the mark. How would it work for the three sisters to be in business together?

"This place is in such disrepair," said Aunt Ethel suddenly. "Have you even considered how much it will cost to fix it up or where you will get the money?"

"We all plan to contribute from our savings," said Louise.

"From your savings?" Aunt Ethel shook her head. "That sounds very foolish to me. Good grief, ladies, have you really thought this through?"

"We're still discussing a number of things," said Jane.

"But to deplete your savings?" Aunt Ethel scowled at the three of them as if they were under her care. "It sounds very irresponsible to my way of thinking. It makes me wonder what Daniel would think of such an idea."

"Father used to encourage people to follow their dreams," said Alice. But she knew that Aunt Ethel was making a good point about their savings. Really, it was all they had to see them through their final years. Were they being foolish?

"Maybe so," said Aunt Ethel, "But perhaps you would be wiser to consider getting a mortgage on the house. It must be worth something."

"Mortgage the house?" exclaimed Alice.

"And have payments to make?" said Louise. "With interest?"

Jane shook her head. "That doesn't sound to me like anything Father would approve of."

"Father was always opposed to debt of any kind," agreed Alice.

"Hmm, I suppose you're right about that." Aunt Ethel shrugged. "Well, I guess it's your house and your decision. I'm sure nothing I can say will stop you three once your minds are made up."

Alice leaned forward and placed her hand on her aunt's arm. "We do appreciate your concern, Aunt Ethel. But, you're right, this is a decision that we three will have to make on our own. We just wanted you to know."

Aunt Ethel stood now, patted her hair and finally grinned. "Well, I can't wait to tell Lloyd the big news."

The three watched as their aunt hurried out of the kitchen.

"The cat's out of the bag now," Louise said dryly.

"God help us," said Alice. And she meant it.

Chapter Eight

"Well, now that was different," said Louise as the three Howard sisters began to file down the aisle of the chapel toward the front door. "Can't say that I've ever heard the Sermon on the Mount interpreted quite like that."

"Pastor Ley isn't used to preaching," Alice said in a quiet voice. "He did his very best."

"Hello, ladies," said Fred as he and Vera joined them.

"We heard the news about the inn." Vera winked at Alice.

"You and the rest of the town." Jane rolled her eyes. "No need to make any sort of press release now."

Vera laughed. "Maybe it's just as well since the *Acorn Nutshell* won't even be out until Wednesday. It'll be yesterday's news by then."

The Howard sisters proceeded toward the front door, cordially greeting Pastor Ley and Patsy. Then they slowly made their way down the front steps. Members of the congregation paused to wave or greet them, most of them reiterating how much they missed Pastor Daniel.

"Sometimes you don't know what you have until it's

gone," Jane whispered into Alice's ear. Alice nodded as she waved to her young orderly friend from the hospital.

"It's just not the same without Pastor Daniel," Ron White told her as they stood outside on the walkway. "For that matter, neither is work without you. When are you coming back, Alice?"

Alice smiled. "Next week. And I'm sure you'll have all sorts of messes for me to sort out by then."

"Hey, I've been trying to keep everything running smoothly while you were gone."

"I'm sure you have." She was about to introduce the young man to her sisters when Florence Simpson pushed her way over to her.

"Alice!" she said in her no-nonsense voice. "What is this I hear about turning Pastor Daniel's house into a *hotel*?"

Alice forced a stiff smile, noticing that other conversations had suddenly quieted down as those standing nearby leaned in closer so that they could hear her response. "Oh no, it's not going to be a hotel, Florence, just a small inn that will cater to—"

"I'm surprised at you, Alice. And you on the church board too. I'd have expected that you'd present this idea for approval before jumping into some kind of harebrained scheme." Florence eyed Jane and Louise as if she suspected they might actually be the masterminds behind this diabolical plan.

Alice blinked. "Why would we need approval for—"

"It *is* the late Pastor Daniel's home, Alice. It *is* a part of the chapel, not to mention an—"

"Excuse me," said Louise as she gave Florence her stern music-teacher look. "Our home is not owned by the chapel."

Alice tossed Louise a glance, as if to warn her against engaging with someone like Florence. But Louise continued. "Our home has never been owned by the chapel. In fact it was Mother's family, the Berrys, who originally donated the land for the chapel in the first place."

Florence glared at Louise now. "I wasn't suggesting that the chapel actually *owned* the Grace Chapel house, I'm simply saying that it's like a part of the chapel and I believe the chapel should've been considered first."

"Opening an inn next to the chapel won't change anything," Alice used her most reassuring tone. "Perhaps guests at the inn will wish to attend services. It could be something of a ministry, and Father always said—"

"But it's a commercial operation!" snapped Florence. "It's like—like money changing in the temple!"

Jane just walked away.

"It's our way of preserving our home," defended Alice. "Using it as an inn will provide an income to keep it up."

Louise shook her head, hooked her handbag over her

arm and went over to join Jane, who was now talking with the Humberts.

"Well, I'm calling an emergency board meeting," said Florence. "I expect you to be there, Alice."

"Of course, I'll be there." Alice sighed. "I'm always there."

Now Florence smiled, but her gray eyes looked as hard as flint. "Good. Perhaps we'll be able to talk some sense into you after all."

Alice could think of no gracious response to this and so she said, "Have a nice day, Florence," and then turned away to join her sisters and the Humberts.

"How could you take that from her?" demanded Jane.

Alice shrugged. "Florence is a little opinionated."

"Opinionated?" Louise shook her head. "That woman is a steamroller."

"She's not as bad as she seems." Alice glanced over to some of the church members and smiled feebly, as if to assure them that all would be well.

"Board meeting this week?" asked Fred.

Alice nodded.

Vera laughed. "Well, that should be fun."

"Maybe it'll all blow over by then," said Jane.

Fred grinned. "Been a while since you lived in a small town, eh, Jane?"

"Now don't you go trying to scare Jane," warned Alice.

"These community squabbles are like a tempest in a teapot—nothing to get worked up over."

Then Jane laughed. "Actually, I find it somewhat amusing."

"I don't." Louise pressed her lips tightly together. "That woman gets my hackles up. Makes me almost forget I'm a good Christian woman."

Pastor Ley and his wife Patsy dropped by the house later in the afternoon to tell Alice about the recently scheduled board meeting. "Florence has, well, sh-she's already called the others," said Pastor Ley as they stood together on the front porch. "I th-thought you should know. It's set for Tuesday evening at seven."

Alice nodded. "That's fine."

He put his hand on her arm. "I'm s-sorry, Alice. I—uh—I don't know why she's making this into such a, you know, an issue. I can't really . . . I mean how w-would an inn next door to the chapel change anything?"

"It won't," said Patsy. "I happen to think it'd be nice to have an inn in the town. Our home isn't very big, and there are times we'd love having someplace where family members could stay during visits and holidays."

"Really?" Alice felt hopeful.

"Yes, I think it's a fine idea."

"I hope the rest of the board will see it like that."

Pastor Ley frowned. "Well, now, I'm not too s-sure. I—uh, I already heard that Lloyd Tynan is p-putting up some resistance."

"It figures." Alice bent down to pet Wendell as he rubbed against her legs. "Lloyd is always saying how the best thing we can do with Acorn Hill is to keep the outsiders out and keep everything exactly the same."

"Well, don't you worry about it," said Pastor Ley. "Cast your c-cares on Him, Alice, for He cares for you."

"Thanks, Pastor."

Alice told the couple good-bye, then sat on the porch swing and waited for Wendell to leap into her lap. "So, what do you think about all this, old boy?" she asked as she scratched the top of his velvety head. She wondered what her father would think. She hoped that he'd enjoy seeing his daughters reunited in a project like this, but what would he think about a church squabble resulting from their decision to open an inn? She searched her heart. Should she have taken this idea to the church board first or was Florence Simpson just being a busybody? Finally, she realized that only God knew these answers. So she took her questions to Him and asked for Him to lead and guide her.

"This a private party?" asked Jane as she stepped out to the porch with a tea tray complete with slices of the banana bread she had baked earlier this morning. She had changed from her church clothes into a pair of loose linen pants and a shirt that looked like it was made out of patchwork pieces and old lace. Combined with her big hoop earrings, they gave her a slightly Bohemian look. Alice had always admired Jane's distinctive sense of style.

Alice grinned. "Not at all."

"Well, I just had to tell someone the good news, and Louise is taking a nap right now."

"What's up?"

"I've been on the phone for most of the afternoon. First I talked to my roommate. Remember I told you about the woman I've been living with since the divorce. Anyway, Sharon is so supportive of my decision to move back home that she's actually offered to box up my stuff and ship it out here for me. Most of my big things were already in storage anyway, and I'll just deal with those later. For now, I think I'll just cash in my return ticket and stay put. I've already called the restaurant and explained everything to my boss. Naturally, Trent wasn't too thrilled to hear that I'm not coming back, but he was really sweet about it. He said he totally understood— that he'd been expecting something like this for some time."

"Really?"

"He said everyone there suspected that I was perfectly miserable, and he just hoped this move would make me happier."

"Do you think it will, Jane?" Alice felt slightly uneasy now. What if Florence's assault on the inn idea had dampened Jane's enthusiasm or even harmed their future business in any way?

Jane reached over and took Alice's hand. "I'm already happier. Just being here with my family is good medicine. I've even been sleeping better. I guess I didn't realize how much I missed you guys until I got out here."

"I've missed you too."

"Alice, I want to apologize."

"Apologize? For what?"

"I should've come home sooner. You know, I almost did—dozens of times during the past year. But the idea of sitting down in front of Father and telling him what a complete failure my marriage had been . . . well, I just couldn't make myself do it. I know that it was completely selfish. And I know that it probably hurt you too. I'm so sorry. I hope you can forgive me."

Alice reached over and hugged her sister. "All is forgiven, Jane."

Jane poured tea for the two of them. "Do you think this Florence is going to be much of a threat?"

"I sure wouldn't want her for our inn's PR representative."

Jane laughed. "Well, I think you're the perfect person to deal with someone like her, Alice. Honestly, I've never seen anyone so calm and controlled as you can be. What a gift you have. You probably should've been a pastor's wife."

"Or a pastor's old maid daughter."

"You're not old enough to be an old maid yet," said Jane.

Alice laughed. "Just how old must one be to qualify?"

"One foot in the grave, I'd guess. If you don't believe me you can ask Aunt Ethel."

Alice nodded. "Yes, I've endured that speech a time or two."

"But really, Alice, you are such a diplomat."

She smiled. "Well, Father always did call me his little peacemaker."

Jane nodded. "Yeah, you're the peacemaker, and I'm the troublemaker."

"No," said Alice firmly. "I'm the peacemaker, and you're the cake-baker." She grinned as she held up a moist slice of banana bread, then took a big bite.

Jane leaned back in the swing and sighed. "Louise must be the music-maker then. So we've got a peacemaker, cake-baker, music-maker—kind of a nice ring to it, don't you think?"

"Sounds like a good combination to me."

Chapter Nine

$\mathcal{T}$uesday night came quickly, and with it the board meeting. Alice walked to the chapel with mixed feelings. On one hand, she had spent the past two days listening to Louise and Jane's indignation about any church opposition. They both felt strongly that the board should have absolutely no say in their business ventures. Of course, Alice didn't disagree with them on this, and yet she wanted to honor her father and the church that he had so lovingly served during the course of his lifetime.

"God, please lead me," she prayed as she walked down the dimly lit hallway toward the meeting room. "And, please, guide my words. 'Let my speech be with grace and seasoned with salt that I may know how to answer any man'—or woman, for that matter." She opened the door and walked into the room.

"Hello, Alice," called Lloyd Tynan. "We've been waiting for you."

She glanced at her watch to see that she was nearly five minutes late—highly unusual for her, but then her sisters had been giving her lots of last-minute advice. "Sorry, I must've lost track of the time."

"No matter," said Pastor Ley kindly. "You're here now."

"Let's call this meeting to order," announced Fred. He had been acting as board chairman for the past several years and so far no one had challenged him for the seat, although Alice suspected that Florence was considering it. For now it was a relief to have Fred in charge. Alice slipped into the vacant chair next to him and stared blankly at the chalkboard. The assembly room was also used for Sunday school, and a Bible verse was still neatly inscribed across the dark board in bright yellow chalk. "Do unto others as you would have them do unto you." Jesus' words sounded simple enough, and yet it seemed that no one ever fully mastered them. At least no one that Alice knew, although her father had come mighty close.

"Well, we all know why I called this emergency meeting," began Florence as she pushed back her chair to stand. Alice could tell that the portly older woman had groomed herself especially for their meeting tonight, donning a red and blue striped polyester dress and gold-toned jewelry, while Alice had simply worn her best jeans and a neat cotton sweater. Florence held up her notes and cleared her throat as if she were about to perform "Ave Maria." Then she began to speak. "The board is called to a meeting tonight because the chapel needs a platform on which to voice its concerns over the use of the parsonage—"

"Excuse me, Florence," interrupted Fred. "But the Howard home is *not* a parsonage. The word *parsonage* suggests that it is owned by the chapel. The Howard home is, and always has been, a private home." He glanced over to Pastor Ley's wife, who although not a board member, always came along to take notes. She nodded to Fred, then returned to her notepad.

"Well, if you want to get technical. It's come to our attention that Pastor Daniel's home—"

"Excuse me again, Florence." Fred gave her a sharp look this time. "Pastor Daniel is deceased and the family home now belongs to his three daughters, Alice, Louise and Jane. How about if we refer to it as the Howard home for the purposes of tonight's meeting?"

"Fine," she snapped. "The *Howard home*. Now, may I please continue?"

"By all means."

"The *Howard home* has always been a good neighbor to Grace Chapel and the chapel has always appreciated this relationship, but it has come to the board's attention that this is about to be drastically changed. We all understand that this private home, a historic home, is about to be turned into a commercial business. Furthermore, the church board had not been consulted in regard to this change." She peered down at Alice. "Isn't that true, Alice Howard?"

"We never really had the chance to consult anyone. My sisters and I only decided to look into the possibility of opening an inn during the past weekend. We hadn't intended for the word to leak out like it did." She glanced at Lloyd Tynan and Aunt Ethel, and then continued. "If we'd known that the board felt a need to be consulted, we surely would've done so. But everything happened so fast, it was actually a bit of a surprise—"

"It was quite a surprise to us too," said Florence indignantly. "Another concern is that we've heard that you intend to use the name of the chapel for your hotel?"

"Excuse me," said Fred with a scowl. "I do not believe the Howard sisters are opening a *hotel.*"

Alice nodded. "That's right, Fred. It's only going to be an inn, a very small inn, in fact, more like a bed and breakfast."

"Nonetheless," continued Florence, "Is this true? Do you plan to call your *inn* Grace Chapel?"

"We liked the sound of Grace Chapel Inn," said Alice weakly. "We never imagined that it would pose any kind of a problem."

"Do you think it's proper to use the name of the Lord's house to promote a business—and right next door?" Florence asked.

Alice considered this. "I suppose I hadn't actually thought of it like that. I guess I thought that it was a compliment to the chapel and perhaps even a way to memorialize my father. But maybe we should reconsider—"

"Hold on there," said Pastor Ley. "B-before you go reconsidering—well, let's kick it around s-some. I don't see any p-problem with sh-sharing the name. I've heard towns-folk call the Howard home 'Grace Chapel house' for ages. I'm certain there are p-people in Acorn Hill who b-believe that's the actual name."

"That's true," agreed Fred. "Most folks do call it the Grace Chapel house. Seems it would be less confusing for everyone if they just stuck with that name."

"Not so fast," said Lloyd. Alice had noticed that both he and Aunt Ethel had been unusually quiet so far, but she'd also suspected it wouldn't last for long. Lloyd stood up now, posturing himself as if he were about to give a formal speech. "If I may remove my church board cap for a moment, I would like to address this group as the mayor of Acorn Hill."

"Feel free," said Fred.

"Well, first of all, as your mayor, I must point out that the city will definitely have some concerns about this *inn business*. For starters, we have some unresolved designation and code issues to be worked through. Now, I haven't had much of a chance to officially investigate anything yet, but

I'm guessing that the Howard home has been designated for low-density residential use."

"But it's not in a strictly residential neighborhood," pointed out Fred. "Thanks to the presence of the chapel."

"True enough. But even so, we'll still have some code issues to go over, then there's business licensing and safety inspections and whatnot." He hooked his thumbs into the lapels of his pale blue suit and smiled contentedly. "If it makes any of you feel better, Grace Chapel Inn is still nothing more than a pipe dream."

Alice's heart sank, but she remained quiet.

"May I speak?" asked Aunt Ethel.

"Go right ahead," said Fred.

Aunt Ethel stood and looked around the group. "As both a neighbor and church board member, I'd like to go on record as having some serious reservations about this little venture. Goodness knows, I don't want strangers traipsing in and out of my neighborhood at all hours of the day and night. And what about the additional traffic? Not to mention, where are the guests going to park their vehicles while they're visiting? And what if they have noisy children or unruly pets? I certainly have no desire to see my neighborhood, or for that matter the chapel's neighborhood, turned into a three-ring circus."

"We have no intention of creating a circus," said Alice.

Suddenly she wished she had her sisters here to back her up. "We only want to make our home into a nice, quiet, dignified place where people will come to rest and reflect—to enjoy the quaint charm of our little town and maybe even attend the chapel. Jane will prepare lovely breakfasts, and Louise will grace us with an occasional evening of classical piano. Is there really anything terribly wrong with that?"

Fred smiled. "I think it sounds wonderful."

"So do I," said the normally quiet and reserved Mr. Overstreet.

Alice turned to see the little old man in the well-worn tweed jacket. He was leaning back in his chair with his arms folded across his front, but he had what seemed a pleased smile on his face.

She blinked in surprise. "You do?"

He nodded. "Yes, I do. I think Pastor Daniel would've approved of this idea as well."

Alice remembered how Mr. Overstreet and her father had enjoyed an occasional game of chess, and she knew how much her father respected this soft-spoken man, but she'd never actually heard the elderly man utter more than a handful of words at once. "Thank you, Mr. Overstreet. Your opinion means a lot to me."

"I'm sure it does," said Florence with open exasperation. "But the rest of us are still not convinced."

Fred nodded. "Perhaps it's time to put this thing to a vote."

Naturally, Florence wasn't ready to let the board vote just yet. She had numerous other concerns she felt she must voice, which she did, as did Aunt Ethel and Lloyd, but finally it seemed that everyone had had his say.

"All right now," said Fred, glancing over at Patsy, who'd been furiously writing down all their comments. "If we're ready, I'd like to motion that we put the matter to a vote now."

"I second," said Mr. Overstreet, surprising Alice again.

"Okay. All in favor of welcoming Grace Chapel Inn into the neighborhood, please raise your hands."

Alice, Fred, Pastor Ley, and Mr. Overstreet raised their hands.

"Opposed?"

Now Florence, Lloyd, and Aunt Ethel raised their hands. Patsy wasn't really on the board and therefore wasn't eligible to vote, although Alice felt certain hers would have been in the affirmative.

Alice tried not to appear too pleased. And she also tried not to feel betrayed by her own aunt. After all, Aunt Ethel did have some valid concerns that Alice would attempt to address later, in private. Mostly Alice was relieved that, thanks to Mr. Overstreet, the majority was in favor of opening the inn.

"Thank you all very much," she directed this to the favorable votes. To the others she said, "I want you to know that my sisters and I are very interested in hearing and addressing your concerns. We have no desire to alienate ourselves from anyone in the community or from our beloved chapel. Be assured that we will most definitely go through all the proper channels to establish our inn. All of your comments and suggestions will be most welcome. Thank you for coming tonight." Then she stood and left.

The night air felt comfortingly cool against her flushed face. She most definitely did not enjoy being in the center of a controversy like this. She hoped that tonight's meeting would be the worst of it. Although, after hearing the mayor's comments, not to mention Aunt Ethel's "neighborly" concerns, she wasn't entirely sure. At least tonight was a small victory. She couldn't wait to tell the good news to her sisters.

"Thank you, God!" she whispered as she hurried up the steps to the porch.

Alice tried to play down Aunt Ethel's opposition to the inn, but Louise finally pinned her down. "Tell it to us straight, Alice, did Aunt Ethel actually vote against the opening of the inn?"

Alice held up her hands. "She did, but then I assured her that we'd listen to her concerns. She will be our closest neighbor and—"

"I cannot believe our own aunt would betray us like that," said Jane.

"Well, I think Alice is right," said Louise. "We need to convince Aunt Ethel that the inn poses no threat to anyone." She shook her head. "I'd much rather have Aunt Ethel for us than against us."

"I agree," said Alice. "Aunt Ethel and Lloyd Tynan could prove to be formidable foes."

"Okay," said Jane. "Let's get a plan together. Louise, you work on Lloyd, and I'll work on Aunt Ethel. I do love her and I'm sure she still has a bit of a soft spot for me." Jane winked at Louise. "And Lloyd certainly took a liking to you the other day."

"Don't be silly." Louise waved her hand. "Just the same, I'll talk to Lloyd about the city business. I'll tell him that I need someone smart and knowledgeable to help me work my way through all the local red tape."

"Great idea," said Jane.

"I guess I'll just continue my role as peacemaker—that and keep praying a lot," Alice said.

"Sounds like a surefire plan for success," said Louise.

Chapter Ten

*O*n Wednesday nights, while most of the chapel parishioners attended a worship service in the sanctuary, Alice met in the basement with the ANGELs, a girls' club that Alice had started years ago. The group's real name, hidden within the acronym, was kept strictly secret. Only the ANGELs and Alice knew exactly what those letters stood for, but they were always quick to point out that it didn't have anything to do with being excessively good or saintly or even angelic, although they did encourage each other toward loving God and performing good deeds.

The girls loved getting together with Alice and always had a good time doing various projects in the chapel's assembly room. The fruits of their youthful energy and enthusiasm were always bestowed upon whomever the ANGELs determined to be the most appreciative recipient, but the actual giving was always done anonymously—and that, the ANGELs all agreed, is what made it so much fun.

"Hey, Miss Howard, are you really going to turn the Grace Chapel house into a hotel?" asked Ashley Moore as she pressed another fabric piece onto her cardboard box. Their current project was creating "treasure" boxes that they would decorate tonight and then fill with cookies the following week.

Alice handed a bottle of glue to Sarah Roberts as she considered her answer. "Well, it's not actually going to be a hotel, Ashley. If everything works out, it'll be just a very small inn—a bed and breakfast."

"Cool," said Sarah. "My mom said we need something like that in Acorn Hill."

Alice smiled. It was always such a relief when she heard someone say anything positive about the possibility of developing an inn. It had been more than a week since the word had "leaked" out, and most of the town seemed either somewhat reserved or totally opposed to their business plan. But Alice suspected this was most likely because they were misinformed. And this, she figured, had to do with folks like Lloyd Tynan and, of course, her own aunt.

Jane and Louise's plans to work on these two had been put slightly on hold when Louise suddenly decided to return to Philadelphia the week before. She felt it was time to get her affairs in order so that she could complete her transition to Acorn Hill. It took her most of a week to finish up her business and pack up her things, but because of her superior organizational skills, all this turned out to be a relatively easy accomplishment.

In the meantime, Jane had decided it might benefit their cause to write an accurate press release that would help set the town straight on their proposed inn. That piece had appeared in the *Acorn Nutshell* just today, along with a grainy photo of the three sisters standing on the front porch. Louise, just back from Philadelphia, had seen the article and had complained that the shot made her look heavy, but Alice thought it wasn't too bad. At least, they were all smiling. Carlene Moss, the *Nutshell's* photographer/reporter/editor/marketer, had even offered to write a story when some of the renovations were actually begun.

"It'll be interesting for the town to follow the progress of the inn," she had said. Fortunately Carlene was one of the few who actually supported growth and development in their small municipality. "As long as it's thoughtful and well planned," she added quickly, as if they might want to quote her. But the sisters had assured Carlene they were in perfect agreement on this. They had no intention of creating an inn if it couldn't be something the whole town would be proud of.

Alice opened another box of sequins and poured them out onto the craft table. The ANGELs oohed and aahed as they picked out their favorite colors and continued with their gluing.

"My dad said that one of your sisters is going to start giving piano lessons," said Jenny Snyder as she glued a silver button onto the lid of her ornate box. "I've always wished I could learn to play."

"Yes, that's my older sister," said Alice. "Her name is Mrs. Smith, and she's a very accomplished pianist. She's taught piano for years. You should look into it before she gets a waiting list."

"I want to learn to play too," said Ashley.

"Me too," added Sarah quickly.

Alice laughed as other girls chimed in. It seemed that all the ANGELs wanted to learn piano. "Well, if you're serious, you girls better talk to your parents and get yourselves signed up." Soon all the ANGELs were discussing what they would do when they became famous concert pianists.

Alice smiled to herself as she went to the kitchen to put out their snack of Jane's homemade snickerdoodles and fruit punch. Despite the negativity running amuck in Acorn Hill right now, she had known she could count on her ANGELs to lift her spirits tonight. Once again, she thanked God for these girls and she prayed that she would continue to be a worthy leader to them.

"Next week, I've invited my sister, Ms. Howard, to join us," she announced toward the end of their meeting. "She's an excellent chef who used to cook for one of San Francisco's finest restaurants—"

"San Francisco, California?" asked Ashley, obviously impressed.

"That's right. She made these cookies tonight, but next week she'll teach us how to make some very special cookies."

"Do we get to eat any of them?" asked Jenny.

"Of course." Alice laughed. "You know our rule."

"Don't muzzle the ox as he treads the grain," quoted Sarah with a quick smile.

Finally Alice checked them on last week's memory verse from Scripture. They all had it nearly word perfect, and she rewarded each of them with a silver angel pencil. Alice had discovered several catalogs over the years from which she'd been able to order lots of inexpensive "angel" treats. Father had offered to have the chapel cover this expense, but Alice had always refused. She didn't mind purchasing these items, because it made it seem more like these were "her girls." Even years down the line it wasn't surprising for a young woman to stop Alice on the street and say, "Hey, remember me, Miss Howard? I used to be an ANGEL."

As much as Alice loved her ANGELs, she was eager to get back home tonight. Louise had only returned from Philadelphia late this afternoon and the three sisters barely had time to catch up. So as soon as the last girl said good night, Alice grabbed her jacket and headed for home.

To her surprise, Aunt Ethel was sitting in the kitchen having tea with Jane and Louise. Aunt Ethel had been keeping something of a low profile during the past week, although Jane had been trying to reach out to her. Perhaps she had made some progress after all.

"Hello, Alice," said Aunt Ethel. "I noticed that Louise was back and thought I should pop in and pay my respects."

"Yes," said Louise. "We've just been catching up."

"Would you like a piece of cheesecake, Alice?" offered Jane.

"Maybe just a small one—"

"A small one?" Aunt Ethel made a face. "How can you only have a small one? Do you know anyone who makes better cherry cheesecake than our own Jane?"

Alice smiled. "No, but that's just the problem. With Jane cooking all this tempting food I'm sure I won't be able to fit into my uniform before long."

"Speaking of your uniform," said Louise, "did you see about cutting back your hours yet?"

"I talked to my administrator yesterday, but I have to admit I'm still not too sure about this idea."

"But you said yourself that you're afraid you've been getting too busy lately," reminded Louise.

"And with the ANGELs and the church board and now the inn," added Jane, "we don't want you collapsing on us."

Alice nodded. "Yes, I'm sure you're probably right. It's just that not too much is happening with the inn yet."

"Well, that's all about to change," announced Louise. "I have an appointment with the city tomorrow and—"

"Oh!" said Jane. "I completely forgot to tell you. Fred called this afternoon and said that a new contractor has just moved into town. He was picking up some supplies at the hardware store, and he and Fred got talking. Fred said it sounds like he knows everything there is to know about renovating historic homes." Jane jumped up and went over to the notepad by the telephone. "Let's see . . . his name is Jim Sharp, and he and Fred plan to come by tomorrow afternoon to have a look around."

"Perfect," said Louise. "We can get the wheels rolling right away."

"What about getting approval from the city?" asked Aunt Ethel.

"We're only talking about renovations right now," said Jane. "While I'm sure we'll need some building permits, I can't imagine why the city wouldn't let us fix up our own home."

"Well, I suppose you're right." Aunt Ethel set down her teacup.

"Is that okay with you, Alice?" asked Jane. "I didn't mean to jump the gun, but it seemed so providential that this contractor should move to town just when we were about to—"

"Maybe it's an answer to your prayers, Alice," said Louise. "You have been keeping up your end in that department, haven't you, dear?"

"Of course." Alice frowned. "I just wish I could be here tomorrow to meet him."

"Can you get off work at two?"

Alice shook her head. "I don't see how. We're a little shorthanded as it is right now."

"Okay then, how about if Louise and I check him out, and if we think he seems all right, then we can arrange for you to meet him later. How's that?"

Alice nodded. "That sounds fine."

"Well, I just hope you girls don't go and get the cart before the horse," warned Aunt Ethel. "No sense putting good money into this decrepit old place if you can't get it back again someday. Bad stewardship, if you ask me. Like pouring water down a rat hole."

Alice studied Aunt Ethel for a moment. She really didn't want to hurt the older woman's feelings, but at the same time she felt she needed to make a strong point here. "Aunt Ethel," she began carefully. "I can understand why you don't feel any special emotional attachment to our house, but—"

"Oh, that's not it, dear. Your father, my beloved brother, made this his home for years. Of course, I have feelings for it."

"That's good," Alice continued. "So maybe you can understand a little bit of what we feel. You need to consider that this house was also our mother's family home. The Berry family built this house in the 1890s, and because of that connection, it probably has even more meaning to us. You see it was our actual blood relatives—on our mother's side—who built and first loved this house." She glanced at her sisters. "I guess I can't speak for Jane and Louise, but this place is very special to me."

Louise nodded. "I couldn't agree more."

"Count me in too," added Jane.

"So you see," said Alice, "renovating our home doesn't feel like a waste of money to us." She shook her head vehemently. "Naturally, we hope that we'll be able move along and that the city will grant us permission to create a nice little inn here, but we'll just have to take it one day at time."

"Bravo!" said Jane.

"Here, here!" added Louise.

"Well." Aunt Ethel stood up. "Thank you for the tea and cheesecake, Jane. It's getting late. I should be turning in."

"Goodnight, Aunt Ethel," they called after her.

The next afternoon, at two o'clock, Alice said a special prayer for Jane and Louise as she replaced old Mrs. Anderson's IV fluid. The elderly woman was sleeping soundly now, a result of her pain medication. She had tripped over a hose in her front yard and broken her hip just a few days ago. A broken hip was bad news for anyone, but particularly troublesome to someone in Mrs. Anderson's age bracket. It seemed that more often than not, an elderly person rarely made it out of hospital care after suffering this particular injury. She hoped that dear Mrs. Anderson would fare better. So as soon as she finished praying for her sisters, she gently laid her hand on Mrs. Anderson's arm and prayed for the little white-haired woman. "Dear heavenly Father, please help Mrs. Anderson to heal quickly and completely. Please protect her from any further complications. And as she's healing, I pray that You would comfort and encourage her, and remind her of how much You love her. Amen."

Alice felt more tired than usual when she parked her car in the driveway by the carriage house. Maybe her sisters were right, maybe she should seriously consider cutting back her hours now. Many nurses began looking into retirement at her age, but Alice had envisioned herself continuing full-time nursing for at least another decade. Had she been unrealistic? She headed up the walk and then stopped and looked up. She noticed that the leaves were turning color now. Their maple tree had various shades of gold and orange and russet illuminated by the late afternoon sun. This colorful sight alone was enough to invigorate her.

"Alice!" called Jane from the porch. "Good news."

Alice hurried up the steps. "Oh, Jane, did you see the fall colors starting to come on?"

Jane nodded. "Yes, isn't it glorious! Father always loved this time of year. It makes me want to get out my easel."

"You should do that, Jane."

"Is that Alice?" called Louise from the doorway.

"Yes, we're coming inside now," yelled Jane as she nearly pulled Alice into the house.

"Did you tell her?" asked Louise.

"Not yet." Jane led Alice into the parlor before she made her sit down in the overstuffed green chair. Alice glanced around the slightly shabby room with surprise. She hadn't actually sat down in here in ages.

"What?" demanded Alice. "What is going on?"

"The contractor," declared Louise dramatically. "It's amazing—as if he's been sent by God."

Alice blinked. "By God?"

Louise laughed. "Well, that's probably a bit presumptuous. But this man knows absolutely everything about old houses. Goodness, you should've heard him explaining this and that to Fred and us."

"But here's what's even better," said Jane. "He really needs work right now, so he's willing to give us a good deal."

"What did Fred say?" asked Alice.

"Fred seems to think Jim's pretty good. He asked him a lot of tough questions and didn't stump the man once."

"So when do I meet him?" Alice asked.

"He was going home to prepare a bid that he'll submit to us," said Jane. "Jim promised to get right on it and he's even going to check with the city about permits and find out about Acorn Hill's restrictions for historic preservation."

"Then he'll be back here with everything by Saturday morning," said Louise.

"Wow." Alice shook her head.

"If we agree to his terms, he can start work on Monday."

"Wow again."

"That's not all," said Louise. "I met with Lloyd Tynan today, and he seems to be a perfectly reasonable person." She fingered her strand of pearls. "He helped me to get some forms for permits and, well, all sorts of things. He actually seems to know more about this town than anyone."

Alice grew hopeful. "Did it seem like he was softening up some? I mean in regard to the inn?"

Louise nodded. "I'm guessing that it's only a matter of time before he comes completely around."

Jane's eyebrows lifted slightly. "He'd better not come around too much, Louise. Aunt Ethel might get jealous."

"That's true," said Alice. "You don't want to forget that he and Aunt Ethel have been, well, you know, dating."

Louise chuckled. "Oh, I know that. It's not as if I'm interested in the man on a personal level. But, certainly there's nothing wrong with enjoying one another's company while we work out our business and zoning issues with the city."

"I guess not." Alice still wasn't entirely sure. "But I wouldn't want to see Aunt Ethel hurt."

Louise patted her on the hand. "Nor would I, dear."

"Speaking of Aunt Ethel," said Jane, "I think we made some serious progress today. I invited her in for some butternut squash soup and I actually believe she's starting to warm up to the idea of an inn. I started telling her about all the social opportunities the inn might provide, an occasional dinner or tea, small piano concerts, private parties and receptions. I've even suggested that there might be some sort of role for her to play in all this."

"You didn't?" said Louise.

"Well, you never know," said Jane. "I'm sure we could think of something to keep her busy and out of trouble. Good grief, you know she'll be popping in and out of here anyway once things get going. We might as well plan ahead and try to put her to some good use."

"Just as long as she doesn't try to take over," said Louise.

Alice tried to let all this new information sink into her brain. It seemed that they had suddenly been moved into the fast lane. Just considering the changes that might be coming their way made her feel tired all over again. She sighed. "Well, I think I'll give my notice to go part time tomorrow."

"Oh, good for you!" said Jane.

"Yes," agreed Louise. "We're going to need your level head around this place. Once renovation begins, there will be lots of decisions to make."

"Oh yeah," said Jane. "I told Jim that we all wanted to pitch in as much as possible. That will save us some money as well as make things go faster."

Louise looked slightly stunned. "You mean *pitch in* as in wielding a hammer or a paint roller?"

Jane nodded. "That too much for you, Louise?"

Louise's face puckered with distaste. "Well, I've just never . . ."

"There's a first time for everything, sis." Jane grinned mischievously.

Louise peered down at her long-fingered pianist hands and just shook her head. "I'm not so sure about this . . . I suppose I might give it a try . . . " Still, she did not seem the least bit convinced.

"I wouldn't mind helping out when I'm not at work," offered Alice. "I painted my bedroom a few years ago and I thought it was rather fun. Although I must admit that I'm not terribly fast."

"But you did a good job," said Jane.

Louise blinked. "You actually painted that room all by yourself?"

Alice nodded. "I'm sure there will be some ways you can help out too, Louise."

Louise still didn't look too confident, but she did promise to give it her best attempt. Then holding up her hand, she repeated their three musketeers' slogan. "All for one and one for all."

Despite her weariness, Alice had to smile. Seeing the three of them united in a cause like this would have so pleased their father. Maybe he was cheering with them right now.

Chapter Eleven

As promised, Jim Sharp showed up on Saturday morning with a briefcase full of impressive-looking paperwork. Alice had to agree that he seemed like a nice enough young man, actually only a few years younger than Jane, but still young by Alice's standards. He seemed to have all the right answers to their questions, yet there was something—Alice couldn't quite put her finger on it—that gave her just the slightest reservation about him.

"I'm not completely sure about Jim," she whispered to Louise as Jane and Jim inspected a portion of dry rot that was weakening one of the front porch's large columns. Jim had thought he could simply replace a portion of the deteriorated post without having to remove the whole thing, but Jane had not been entirely convinced.

"Why not?" Louise asked in a quiet voice as she toyed with a loose edge of wallpaper hanging on the foyer wall. "He seems perfect for us. And besides, where will we find anyone else?"

"There's Clark Barrett," suggested Alice. "He's been working in Acorn Hill for more than forty years now."

"You mean he's not retired yet?" Louise shook her head. "Why, he's nearly as old as I am."

"He's experienced and established in our community," said Alice. "Maybe we should get a second opinion from him."

"And lose time? Jim has already said that if we get a jump on this we can get a good portion of the exterior projects completed before winter sets in."

Alice waited as Jane and Jim came back into the house.

"Well, I think Jim was right," announced Jane as they joined them in the foyer. "I can see now that most of that post is perfectly fine. It's only the bottom few inches that are rotting. And, he's absolutely right, we'll save all kinds of money by not having to replace it." She smiled with satisfaction.

"That's true," said Jim as he slipped a pencil behind his ear. "A post like that would have to be special ordered and specially milled. Not only is it expensive but it takes a long time too."

Jane patted Jim on the back. "So, aren't you glad we found such an expert, Alice?"

Alice nodded mutely. Perhaps she was being too sensitive. After all, Jane and Louise and even Fred had spent more time with Jim than she. They all seemed to think that Jim was the next best thing to sliced bread.

"So, do we have a deal then?" he asked with a broad smile.

"As far as I'm concerned, we do," said Jane.

"I'm certainly in," agreed Louise.

Alice nodded again. "Then so am I."

So they all shook on it before they went into the study to sign the papers.

"I thought perhaps we might open a checking account with the inn's name on it," explained Louise. "That way we can use those funds for renovation expenses and whatnot. It will help us to start keeping all our finances straight, for business records later on."

"That sounds smart," said Jim. "But if I'm going to start on Monday, I'll need a deposit up front by then."

"How much do you require?" asked Jane.

"I usually like half up front and half upon completion, but since this is a fairly good-sized project, we could break it into more payments."

"That would be nice," said Louise. "Perhaps in thirds?"

He nodded. "Thirds would be fine."

Still, Alice felt a little nervous. These were large sums of money they were talking about, most of it Louise's, although she and Jane were contributing as much as they could afford. Still, she could think of nothing concrete to say that would deter them. She had no legitimate reason to put the brakes on this deal. So it was all settled. Louise and Jane both seemed elated over the arrangements.

"We're getting a really good deal," Jane assured her two sisters over a lunch of crab cakes and salad.

"I think so too," admitted Louise with excitement. "I've always enjoyed watching *This Old House* on public television and I've seen just how much these kinds of historic renovations can cost."

"I wish we'd had Fred look at the final paperwork," said Alice.

"Now that's a good idea," said Louise. "It's not too late. I believe there's a three-day recision period for a contract this size. Maybe you should run the papers over to Fred for a second opinion."

"Would that make you feel better?" asked Jane. "You still seem a little uncomfortable with this, Alice."

Alice shrugged. "Oh, I'm sure I'm just being silly, but then I've never had much to do with such large sums of money. Goodness, whenever I buy a car, which certainly hasn't been too often, I tend to fret over the whole transaction for weeks. I suppose I'm just being overly cautious with the house. But if you two don't mind, I'd like to ask Fred to go over it."

Later in the day, she paid Fred a visit at the hardware store, but since it was Saturday and he was having a seasonal sale, he asked if he could take the papers home with him and look them over more carefully later on that evening. Alice felt relieved as she walked down Hill Street. She remembered how her father had often said there was safety in seeking good counsel from a number of friends. Now, feeling as if some of the weight had been lifted from her shoulders, she decided to pop into the Coffee Shop to say hello to Hope.

"That was a nice piece in the paper," said Hope as she set a cup of tea in front of Alice.

"You read it?"

"Of course. Don't you think everyone in town did?"

"I hope so, since that was our goal. We knew there were some rumors floating around that weren't accurate. We hoped that the press release would straighten some people out."

"I think it worked."

"Really? Have you heard anything specific?"

Hope laughed. "Girlfriend, I hear *everything*."

"Oh, of course, but do you maintain client confidentiality?" asked Alice as she glanced around the crowded coffee shop. She was only partially joking.

"No way. This is a public place. If people discuss their problems in here they better want the whole town to hear about it before too long."

"So, tell me then, what is the consensus regarding our little business proposal now?"

"Well, opinions are beginning to improve a bit. Some

people actually like the idea of a good bed and breakfast coming to town." She lowered her voice. "I even heard Betsy Long saying she hoped that locals would be welcome to partake in the breakfasts. Better not let our cook hear me saying that. And, of course, everyone knows we don't have a proper hotel or anything, so a place for visitors to stay appeals to some folks."

"That sounds fairly positive."

"Yeah, but I can't lead you on either, Alice. There are still plenty of people who agree with the mayor when it comes to change of any way, shape or form around here." She shrugged as she wiped down the counter next to Alice. "Remember when Percy Thomas painted his house yellow instead of white? That must've been three years ago and people are still talking about it. I just don't get it. What are folks so afraid of anyway? I happen to think change is good."

"I noticed you changed your hair again," said Alice as she glanced at Hope's almost platinum locks.

Hope grinned and patted her hair. "Yeah, I like to shake people up around here. What do you think of it? Too California?"

"I think it looks good on you. Besides, now you can tell me whether it's true that blondes have more fun."

Hope winked at her. "Too soon to say, but I'll be sure to let ya know when I find out."

Alice paid her check, leaving Hope a nice tip, and then headed across the street to the Nine Lives Bookstore.

"Hi, Alice," called Viola Reed from behind the counter. "Long time no see."

"Don't I know it, but it's been a little busy these last few weeks."

"I'm sure it has. I never actually saw you after your father passed on, but I was sorry to hear about it."

"Thanks," said Alice. "We appreciated the coleslaw you sent over. I guess Louise returned your bowl."

Viola nodded. "You'd think it shouldn't be as hard to lose someone who's getting up there in years, but I'm sure it's still tough. Although it did sound as if he went peacefully enough." She stroked the fat orange marmalade cat that stretched itself across her cluttered counter. "I think it's better to go like that than to waste away in a hospital or nursing home, don't you think?"

"Most definitely. To tell you the truth, that's just the way I'd like to go when my time comes, either like that or in my sleep. I think it'd be great to simply go to sleep and then just wake up to the glory of heaven. My goodness, what a surprise that'd be."

"I guess that's all well and good if you're absolutely certain you're going to heaven—or that there even is a heaven. Being that you're a pastor's daughter, I'm sure you've got this whole thing all figured out, Alice. As for me, well, now, I just don't feel so sure. Maybe it's a good thing I've got nine lives." Viola chuckled as she adjusted a large paisley scarf over her bulky shoulders.

Alice smiled. Everyone in town knew that Viola had experienced several brushes with death—hence the name of her bookstore. Well, that and her love of felines. Despite her near death experiences, Viola still managed to keep herself distanced from both God and the chapel.

"So, how many lives do you estimate you've got left now, Viola?" asked Alice.

"I'd guess I'm down to about four. Course you never know for sure. I can't remember every single thing from my childhood. My mother once told me that I did have a severe case of measles as an infant, although I'm not sure if that was life threatening or not. I might be down to three."

Alice nodded. "Still, the time will eventually come when you'll need to examine what God has to offer you in the hereafter."

Viola laughed. "You're starting to sound more and more like your dad, Alice."

"I'll take that as a compliment."

"And that's just how I meant it." Viola leaned forward on the counter. "I'll tell you what, Alice. When I'm ready to hear about God's plan for my salvation, or whatever it is that you people call it these days, you will be the first one that I call."

"Sounds like a deal." Alice glanced around the crowded shop. "Now, tell me, Viola, have you got any new mysteries in?"

Viola scowled. "Oh, Alice, why do you waste your time on such rubbish?"

Alice shrugged. She knew Viola's strong opinions on popular fiction. "I don't know, Viola, I just enjoy them."

Viola shook her head as she led Alice over to the sparse fiction section. She picked up a hardback book and held it in her hand as if it were unclean. "This is by a new British author who I heard about several months ago. I read an article saying that she was gaining interest in the UK. I figured I'd give her a try, although I must say I'm not impressed."

Alice read the back cover of the first book. "Sounds promising," she said. "I'll take it."

Viola rolled her eyes. "Well, I guess there's no accounting for taste."

So Alice purchased her book and bade Viola good-bye, then went back outside. Just as she was crossing Hill Street she happened to notice a man and woman entering the Coffee Shop. She did a double take. It was her sister Louise accompanied by Lloyd Tynan! *Of course*, Alice assured herself, *the two of them are simply discussing the inn.* But then this was a Saturday, and people in Acorn Hill did like to talk—and sighting the mayor with a woman other than Aunt Ethel could easily set tongues to flapping. *Oh dear, I hope Louise knows what she's doing.*

Alice sent up a silent prayer as she hurried toward home. She didn't like feeling so alarmed over such a seemingly small thing, but she knew better than anyone her own tendency to worry too much about "small things." Her compulsion to fret was also one of the biggest reasons for Alice's fervent and active prayer life. She found herself constantly running to God with her worries—both large and small. She reassured herself that she was doing exactly what the Scriptures taught. Besides, as Vera was kind to point out, perhaps it was simply the way God had made her, a natural result of Alice's very sensitive nature. She just tended to feel things more deeply and intensely than most people. Alice liked to see it in this positive light, but to be perfectly honest, she felt it was both a blessing and a curse.

Right now it troubled her to think that Aunt Ethel might become upset by word of Louise and Lloyd's being together at the Coffee Shop. Like so many other things in life, Alice felt personally responsible for this too. If she hadn't encouraged her sisters to develop the inn, or if she'd simply minded her own business and kept her mouth shut, then her aunt's life would be proceeding happily along, and everything would still be the same as before. But then, Alice wondered, was keeping everything the same really for the best?

Oh dear! She just hoped the three of them weren't getting in over their heads!

Chapter Twelve

*B*y Sunday afternoon, Aunt Ethel's nose was seriously out of joint. Alice suspected this was related to something that had been said at church that morning, probably something about Louise and Lloyd's having been spied at the Coffee Shop the day before. All Alice knew was that Aunt Ethel had turned down Jane's invitation for lunch, and with no explanation whatsoever. This could only mean trouble.

"I say we just let it be," said Jane as she seasoned a large pot of her seafood stew.

"Yes." Louise nodded but maintained her focus on her current knitting project, a white wooly scarf for Cynthia. "Let's just let sleeping dogs lie."

Alice sighed deeply. "Aunt Ethel may appear to be a sleeping dog at the moment, but you better watch out when she wakes up. She's been known to have a pretty sharp bite."

"Well, who's she going to bite?" asked Jane. "Lloyd or Louise?"

"Hard to say—maybe both." Alice tasted the sample that Jane held out to her. "Oh, Jane, that's delicious."

"I've felt Aunt Ethel's teeth before," said Louise. "I'm not the least bit worried."

"Speaking of worries," Jane tossed in another twig of rosemary and replaced the lid on the pot, "what did Fred say about Jim's bid and contract?"

"He seemed to think everything was in order. He agrees with you two that the price is more than fair."

"See?" Louise pointed a knitting needle at Alice triumphantly.

Alice nodded. "Yes, but it makes me feel better to know that."

"Good." Jane slid a pale plump loaf of unbaked wheat bread into the hot oven. "That's one less thing for you to worry about."

"Besides, we have some new things to think about right now." Louise set her knitting aside and reached for a large tapestry bag.

"And that would be?"

Louise ceremoniously set her bag on the kitchen table. She pulled out a notebook and a large deck of paint samples. "I've been gathering a few things to help get us going, and it's time to start discussing paint colors."

"Oh, good," said Jane as she wiped her hands on her apron. "Paint. Now this is right up my alley."

"I think we should start with the exterior colors,"

said Louise. "Since that's the first part of the house that people will see."

"I agree," said Alice. "But what's wrong with keeping it like it is now? I mean it's been that pale peach for as long as I can remember, and it just seems to be fitting. Besides, isn't that a traditional color for this style of house?"

"I tend to agree with you, but I thought we should at least explore the options," said Louise. "I thought perhaps we'd like to paint the trim something other than white this time. Maybe a nice dark green would appear more inviting?"

Jane cleared her throat. "I'm afraid you're both being much too conservative. For one thing, most Victorian homes were never painted in pastels originally. That's something that came along later. Most Victorian era homes were painted in fairly intense, vivid colors—and some wild combinations too. You should see some of the painted ladies in California."

"Painted ladies?" Alice frowned. "That doesn't sound very nice."

"That's what they call them. I've seen purple and green and gold and magenta—and all on the same house."

"Good heavens!" said Louise.

"It does sound rather garish," agreed Alice.

"Some might think so, but the truth is they are historically correct. Once you get used to it, it's really rather warm and friendly looking."

"But purple and green and magenta." Louise gasped. "Certainly you wouldn't want to see our house painted like that, would you, Jane?"

"Well, I'm not opposed to doing a little research to find out the original colors of the Berry home."

"The only photos we have are in black and white," said Alice.

"Yes, but there are paint experts who can photograph chips of the old paint. They use a high-powered microscope, then somehow they put it into a computer in order to discover what color was originally underneath."

Louise looked interested. "Yes, I believe I saw that on *This Old House* once. It seems to me that they finally decided on an awful shade of mustard."

"I happen to think mustard is a nice color," defended Jane.

"But what if our original colors turn out to be horrible?" asked Alice. "The townspeople might throw a fit. Just yesterday, Hope, down at the Coffee Shop, was reminding me of the time when Percy Thomas painted his house yellow. It created such a scandal that you'd have thought he'd shot his mother. Honestly, people were really shaken up."

Jane laughed. "Well, maybe this town needs a little shaking."

Louise looked thoughtful. "Now that I think about it, Lloyd told me how important it would be for us to preserve the historical integrity of our house. Do you suppose he meant the paint colors too?"

"I don't know," said Alice. "But what if it was originally painted hot pink and chartreuse and peacock blue?"

Louise's hand flew over her mouth. "Goodness, you don't think our own relatives would have such ghastly taste, do you?"

Jane shrugged. "You never know."

Alice looked at Jane's tie-dyed T-shirt, a combination of hot pink, teal blue, tangerine and lime green, and then winced. "I'm not saying that I don't like bright colors, Jane, I, uh, I just meant that—"

"Hey, it's okay. I realize that our tastes aren't exactly the same. I just hope we can do what's best for the house and not be complete fuddy-duddies about it."

Louise patted her pearls. "Well, I'm sure I must come across as a fuddy-duddy to you sometimes, Jane, but I prefer to think of myself more as a classic."

"Classic is good," Jane reassured her. "But sometimes a little bit of well-chosen color can really add some energy and life to a place. I don't know about you two, but I'd like our inn to have some individuality and charm. I don't want it to look like a house that belongs to three little old ladies."

"I agree," said Alice. "Even though I love antiques, I'm not really fond of things like lace doilies, tasseled lamps or collections of porcelain figurines that have to be carefully dusted every other day."

Louise frowned as if she were deeply offended now, and Alice realized that, other than mentioning flowered uphol-stery and layers of tablecloths, she had just about perfectly described Louise's home in Philadelphia. In fact, now that Alice thought about it, she felt certain that those sorts of items must be the majority of contents of all those crates that Louise had the moving men cart to the basement for storage last week.

"Oh, Louise," said Alice in her most apologetic tone, "I'm not suggesting that your taste isn't perfectly—"

"Look, it's obvious that all three of us have very dif-fering tastes and styles." Louise fanned open the color deck on the kitchen table. "Perhaps we shouldn't attempt to resolve *that* just yet. Maybe we should simply begin by choosing our interior colors first. I know that I'd love to have my new bedroom's woodwork repainted in a nice shade of green, and perhaps some floral wallpaper. Any objections to *that?*"

"I think we should be free to do whatever we like in our own bedrooms," said Jane as she began poring over the colors, flipping back and forth and pulling out ones that she appeared to like. The sisters had agreed that they would all take rooms on the third floor, leaving the second floor for guests.

"I completely agree," said Alice quickly. "Those spaces should be ours alone to decorate however we please."

"Hmm," Jane pointed to a curious shade of reddish purple. "I think I might like to give this one a try."

Alice blinked at the strong color. "Really, the entire room?"

Jane nodded. "I think it would look fantastic with the golden wood floors and really set off my blond Danish furniture. Then I'll put some of my art on the walls, and voilà, I'll feel right at home."

Louise peered down to read the name of the color. "Oriental Eggplant? Goodness, Jane, are you absolutely certain about this?"

"Yep. I can't wait to break out the paintbrushes."

Alice knew right then that their troubles were only beginning.

By the middle of the following week, it was obvious that some decisions regarding the exterior colors of the house needed to be made soon. Besides, Alice felt that anything would be better than the way their house looked right now. The painters had begun their work by power washing and then sanding and wire brushing the siding until it looked absolutely horrible. Then they had used a variety of primer colors to cover the bare pieces of lap siding—pale shades of gray, green, even blue were now splotched about the house. Talk about a painted lady!

Jim had explained that this was customary, a way to use up leftover paint and save money, but even so it seemed disrespectful to Alice. She felt their old house must be thoroughly embarrassed to be seen in such a state, sort of like the woman who gets locked out in the front yard after slipping out for the newspaper wearing only her faded bathrobe and pink fuzzy slippers. Alice knew for certain that she wouldn't want to stand out there for very long.

"Now, I hate to push you ladies," said Jim one evening just after Alice arrived home from work. "But my paint crew will be done with the prepping and priming by early next week. So unless you want your house to go all winter looking like a great big pinto pony, you'd better give us some paint colors to work with here."

"I sent the paint chips out for analysis on Monday," explained Jane as they gathered around the kitchen table and studied a booklet on historical paints that Jane had sent for on the Internet. "I expect to hear something soon."

"Good." He nodded. "I'm counting on you." Jim winked at her as he tipped his hat and left.

"I think he likes you, Jane," said Louise in a teasing tone.

"Oh, get real!" Jane rolled her eyes as she grated some Parmesan cheese over the salad she had just tossed. "Even if I were ready for something like that, Jim Sharp is definitely not my type."

"Well, anyway, it might make him work harder if he thinks he's impressing you," said Louise.

"Sort of like the way you're impressing Lloyd?" asked Jane.

Alice waited for her older sister's response.

"Goodness, Jane, you certainly don't think I'm *trying* to impress Lloyd, do you?"

Alice cleared her throat. "Well, Louise, that's not exactly how Aunt Ethel sees it."

"Aunt Ethel has actually spoken to you?" asked Jane.

"*When?*" demanded Louise. "We've scarcely seen her all week. Why, I even ran into her at the grocery store and she skittered away like a scared mouse."

"What's up, Alice?" asked Jane.

Alice could tell she had both her sisters' full attention now. She smiled. "Well, if I can take off my shoes and someone will pour me a cup of hot tea, I will tell you both the whole story."

Jane and Louise both scrambled for the teapot and kettle and Alice exchanged her work shoes for a comfortable pair of slippers and, within a matter of minutes, all three sisters were seated around the kitchen table.

"All right, Alice, spill the beans," commanded Louise.

"Well." Alice took a slow sip of the Earl Gray tea before she set down her cup. "Aunt Ethel called me at work this morning. She asked if she could meet me at the hospital for lunch."

"And?" Louise was tapping her fingers on the table with impatience.

"Naturally, I said, sure, why not."

"Come on, Alice!" Jane was losing patience, but Alice was enjoying having the upper hand for a change.

"Aunt Ethel met me in the cafeteria where we both decided to try the blue plate special, which I must say is nothing at all like Jane's delectable lasagna—"

"Alice Christine!" said Louise. "Quit stringing us along."

"Right. So right there in the middle of the noisy hospital cafeteria, Aunt Ethel tearfully informs me that she is certain that she and Lloyd are history now. She is convinced that Louise has permanently stolen his affections and—"

"Oh poppycock!" Louise stood and started to pace across the tiled kitchen floor, fingering her pearls like a rosary with each step.

"Go on," urged Jane.

"Now it seems that Aunt Ethel is considering moving to Potterston."

Louise stopped and looked at Alice. "You're not serious."

"I am."

"What about Aunt Ethel?" asked Jane. "Is *she* serious, or is she just pulling your leg?"

"You can never tell with Aunt Ethel," said Alice. "I've seen her get dramatic over things in the past. Sometimes it's just a bluff, but you can never know for sure. She said she's already found an affordable apartment complex for senior citizens."

Louise sank down into a kitchen chair. "Goodness, I feel absolutely terrible now."

"Aunt Ethel wanted me to ask you something, Louise." Alice couldn't help but suppress a giggle.

Louise scowled. "Well, go ahead, ask me."

"Aunt Ethel wants to know if your intentions toward Lloyd are honorable or not."

"*Honorable?*" Louise blinked. "Were those her exact words, Alice?"

Alice nodded.

"Well, what on earth does she mean by *that?* " Jane shook her head.

Alice laughed, but quickly recovered when she saw Louise's grim face. "I'm sorry, Louise."

"*Honorable?*" Louise exhaled slowly as she shook her head. "Perhaps I've let this thing go too far."

"Didn't you say that Lloyd has already walked you

through most of the city's red tape?" Jane peered at Louise. "Aren't all our permits in process and looking fairly promising now?"

"Yes."

"Then what's going on?" asked Jane.

Louise waved her hand. "Oh, nothing. Nothing whatsoever. Lloyd has turned out to be…well, a very nice friend. Honestly, that is absolutely all there is to it."

"Is that what Lloyd thinks too?" asked Jane.

"Well, now I'm not entirely sure." Louise grew thoughtful. "It's been so long since I've had any kind of involvement, well, of the romantic kind, that I guess it's possible I may have confused the poor man a bit."

"As well as Aunt Ethel," added Alice.

"Dear me, I wonder what I should do now."

"You should tell Lloyd Tynan." Jane went to check on the oven.

"Gently," said Alice. "Let him down gently."

"You're right," agreed Louise. "I'll take care of it at once."

Alice sighed. "Aunt Ethel will be glad to hear of it."

"Should I tell her too?" Louise looked doubtful.

"I don't think so," said Alice. "Somehow I think it might go better with her if she hears it from someone else."

"Trying to protect Aunt Ethel's pride, are we?" Jane closed the oven door and removed her mitt.

"Just her feelings," said Alice. "I know she comes across as a troublesome busybody sometimes, but she is the last of Father's family."

"Good old Alice," said Jane. "Always looking out for everyone else."

Louise excused herself to call Lloyd.

Chapter Thirteen

*A*lice was surprised to discover that she actually liked Jane's new bedroom once the painting and decorating was complete. As it turned out, Oriental Eggplant wasn't nearly as garish as she'd expected.

"It makes the room feel cozy," she admitted when Jane proudly showed it to her. "I like how the dark color makes your art stand out. It reminds me of a gallery."

"That white matting really helps to make the pieces pop, doesn't it."

"Jane!" exclaimed Alice as she examined a painting more closely. "These are your own creations!"

Jane smiled.

"I didn't know you did modern art."

"It was sort of an experimental thing. Remember my therapy phase?"

"Well, I really like them. Do you have more?"

Jane laughed. "Yes. Painting proved to be quite cathartic."

"You should consider a show."

"Here in Acorn Hill?" Jane frowned. "I don't think so."

"Well, maybe we could use some of them in the inn."

"Oh, Alice, do you think Louise would go for it? I would absolutely love to do the dining room in a more contemporary style. It would be so much more like what I was used to back in the city."

Suddenly Alice wasn't too sure about what she was getting herself into. "I guess we'd better talk to Louise about it."

Jane shook her head. "She'll say no."

"What did she think of your room?"

Jane made a face. "I can't remember her exact words, but she sort of stammered and cleared her throat and said something like, 'well, isn't this *interesting.*' I could tell she hated it."

"Oh, I doubt that—"

"Louise and I are as different as night and day, Alice. Honestly, I sometimes wonder how this will ever work. It's good that we have you."

Alice tried not to gulp.

"*Yoo-hoo,*" called Louise. "Are you girls up here?"

"In here," answered Jane. "Alice is checking out my new digs."

"Aunt Ethel just called and said she'd be pleased to join us for dinner tonight."

"So, everything between you two is all right now?" asked Alice.

"I think so. We met for pie this afternoon, and Aunt Ethel gave me a little lecture about men and relationships and propriety." Louise laughed. "Can you imagine—at our age? I had to bite my tongue a number of times."

"And you did?" asked Alice.

Louise nodded. "For the sake of the family, I did."

Jane patted her on the back. "Good girl."

"So what do you think of Jane's décor?" asked Louise, peering at Alice with unmasked curiosity.

"I think it's quite nice." Alice smiled. "It feels cozy and artsy and fun—all at the same time."

Louise nodded, but still looked unconvinced. "Jane has offered to help me paint the trim in my room tomorrow."

"I tried to talk her out of the wallpaper."

Louise shook her finger. "Too late. I already ordered it."

"Speaking of décor," said Jane. "Guess what came by FedEx today?"

"Our paint colors?"

Jane grinned.

"What are they?" asked Alice.

"Yes, Jane, tell us."

"Not until dinner."

"But what about Aunt Ethel?" asked Louise.

"She's family. She has a right to see them too. Besides, it might be wise to have her in on this from the get go."

Alice couldn't stand the suspense. "But are they—"

"No more questions." Jane held up her hands as she moved toward the door. "And unless you two plan to help fix dinner, you better stay out of the kitchen. I don't want you pestering me about the paint colors while I'm trying to concentrate on cooking."

It wasn't until both dinner and dessert were finished and cleared away that Jane finally brought a large brown folder into the dining room. "I'm going to turn the lights up now so that we can get a better look at these colors."

"This is so exciting," said Alice.

"Now who decided on these colors?" asked Aunt Ethel.

"Our ancestors," said Jane. Then Louise brought their aunt up to date on the computer process of uncovering historically accurate colors.

"I don't know about this," said Aunt Ethel. "This house has been peach for as long as I can remember."

"The layers of paint don't lie," explained Jane. "Originally this house was definitely *not* peach. The computer proved this."

"Goodness, isn't technology amazing." Aunt Ethel shook her head.

First Jane pulled a rough sketch of the house from the

folder. "I did this rather quickly," she explained. "It was a guide for where the paint chips had been removed." She pointed to what looked like a key. "A is for the main body. B is for the shutters, and so on."

"Interesting," murmured Aunt Ethel, obviously pleased to be involved.

"I made a copy of my sketch, so that I could color it in according to what the original colors were—just so we could see how it looks all together." Jane paused to look at the three women. "Are you ready?"

They all nodded eagerly and Jane pulled out a second picture of the house. "It's really rather nice," she told them as they all stared. "I mean it's actually quite conservative for a Victorian—"

"What color is *that*?" asked Louise, pointing to the strip of trim along the roof.

Jane laughed. "It looks quite similar to my Oriental Eggplant, doesn't it?"

"The body color isn't too bad," said Alice. "Would you call it sort of a taupe?"

"Maybe a dark taupe, with more hints of brown."

"How about cocoa?"

"That sounds about right. We'll call it cocoa."

"*Tsk-tsk*. It's so dark," said Aunt Ethel. "You can be certain the town will never agree to this."

"They are the accurate historical colors," defended Jane. "I don't see how they can disagree."

Aunt Ethel just shook her head. "But it's so—so—"

"Horrible," added Louise.

"What about the green trim for the shutters?" asked Alice. "You said you like dark green trim, Louise?"

Louise looked like she was about to cry. "Can't we just burn these samples, Jane? Pretend that they never came? Go to good old-fashioned white or even a nice cream?"

Jane pulled out large pieces of painted cardboard now, arranging them on the table. There were four colors in all: cocoa for the body, dark green for the shutters, eggplant for the roof trim and creamy white for the trim around the windows.

Alice studied the colors for a long moment. "They're not really so bad," she finally said.

"*Not so bad?* " Louise looked at Alice as if she'd just used profanity.

"No. They're starting to grow on me. In fact, I think they might actually look friendly."

"*Friendly?*" Aunt Ethel looked as though she thought Alice had completely taken leave of her senses.

"Yes. Now that I think about it, our big light-colored house is a little imposing. The original colors are more humble somehow. They're really growing on me. I think they will make the yard and flowers look more interesting."

"That's exactly right," said Jane, patting Alice on the back. "You seem to have a bit of an artist's eye."

"Oh, I don't know . . ."

"To be honest, I've never been terribly fond of the color," said Jane. "I used to jokingly tell my friends that I lived in the giant peach."

"But it's always been a giant peach," said Louise in a tremulous voice. "Why do we have to change it?"

"Right," said Aunt Ethel. "You've just started to get some support from the town lately. Why do you want to rock the boat now?"

"Because change is good," said Jane.

"And because, in this case," Alice paused to look at the colors again, just to make sure that she was really sure, "I honestly think it'll be an improvement."

"Oh, Alice." Aunt Ethel groaned. "Of all people, I'd think that *you* would want to protect your father's home and keep it just the same."

Alice paused to consider how her father might react to a change of this sort. Despite his years, he had always adapted rather easily to change. Also, he was probably the most humble man that Alice had ever known, and for some reason the new colors seemed inviting and humble to her.

"Well, I can't really speak for Father, but do you want to know what I *think* he might say about this?"

They all nodded and looked very interested.

Alice took a deep breath. "Father was a very humble man. I think that he would be the first to admit that this big three-story house is a bit imposing in the first place, and then to be painted peach . . . although, I'm sure it never occurred to him to change the color since it had been left to him and Mother looking like this. I can imagine that he would've enjoyed living in a more humble home. I suspect he would think returning to the original colors would be an improvement."

Both Aunt Ethel and Louise looked thoroughly disappointed and slightly deflated by Alice's little speech, but neither of them spoke a word.

"Well said, Alice." Jane sighed. "I don't want to make anyone unhappy. It's not as if I personally picked out these colors, but I agree completely with Alice. I think Father would've felt more comfortable in a house that was a little more friendly."

Louise groaned. "Well, I have to agree with you on some points, but isn't there some way we can compromise?"

"Like how?" asked Alice.

"Well, I do like the trim paint, and maybe if the main body color could be just a little lighter, like a nice dignified beige." She shook her head. "But I cannot abide that awful eggplant color."

"The problem with a compromise," said Jane, "is that we instantly lose the historical integrity we were striving for, and that could lead to a battle with the community."

"She's right," said Alice. "If we don't stick to the authentic colors, we'd probably just have to paint it peach again."

"Yes, I suppose that's true." Louise looked defeated. "The rules from the county historic preservation society clearly state that restoration changes must be either historically accurate or approved by the committee."

"Does that mean that we can go ahead with the painting *without* approval?" asked Jane hopefully.

"If it's historically accurate." Louise sighed.

"Just how accurate is this computer company anyway?" demanded Aunt Ethel. "What gives them the right to make these kinds of decisions?"

"They're used by historic renovators all across the country. I have all their information right here, if you'd like to read it, Aunt Ethel."

She waved her hand. "No, thanks. I just wondered."

"So, are we in agreement?" asked Jane. "Jim wants me to order the paint tomorrow so they can begin on Monday."

Louise pressed her lips together for a long moment, then finally said, "I suppose I'll have to agree with the two of you, but now, if you don't mind, I am going to bed with a headache."

"It's a good thing *I* don't have a vote," said Aunt Ethel as she pushed back her chair. "Because I would definitely decline. *Harrumph.* I wonder what the church board will think of this, Alice."

"Oh, Aunt Ethel, do you really think this has anything to do with the church board? Don't you remember what was decided at the last 'emergency' meeting?"

"Well, I'm sure that Florence will be interested in these latest developments. And Lloyd too, for that matter."

Jane turned to Alice and rolled her eyes. "Thanks for coming tonight, Aunt Ethel."

"Thank you for the lovely dinner, Jane. That prime rib was so tender it practically melted in my mouth."

"Thanks." Jane gave her aunt a weak smile and waited until the elderly woman made her way out. "Talk about biting the hand that feeds you," she said to Alice, and they both laughed.

"Don't worry," said Alice. "I'm sure Aunt Ethel will come around before long. She usually does. This will probably blow over with the community too—eventually."

"You mean after the townsfolk finally get used to the new colors, like in a few months?"

"Or years."

Chapter Fourteen

Alice was just finishing up her final rounds at the hospital when she noticed a portly woman hurrying down the hallway toward her. She was too far away to see her face clearly, but her distinctive march was a dead giveaway.

"Alice!" called Florence Simpson, huffing her way toward her. "Have you got a minute?"

Alice closed her clipboard and forced a congenial smile to her lips. "I'm just finishing up, Florence. What can I do for you? Medical emergency?"

"No, no." Florence shook her head and caught her breath. "I was just visiting my great-nephew on my husband's side, tonsillectomy."

"How's young Bradley doing?"

"He's fine. Spoiled rotten, but recovering just fine." Florence lowered her voice. "Now, tell me, Alice Howard, what in the world is going on at your house? Last week it looked like a splotchy mess, but Ethel reassured me at church that it was only temporary. Now I drive by the place today, and it looks like it's the color of dried mud. Were you aware of this?"

Alice smiled. "We prefer to call it 'cocoa.' Actually, we are painting it the historically correct colors, Florence. You know it's listed in the historic register, and these things must be done correctly."

"But muddy brown? How can that be right? Everyone in town knows that the house has always been the peachy color."

Alice shook her head. "Not in the beginning. We are painting it the original colors."

"Well, even if it *was* that color in the beginning—and I'm not even convinced of that, although I suppose it's possible that your ancestors didn't have very good sense—but at least someone in your family had the wits about him to paint it something other than that awful muddy brown? Good night, what could you people have been thinking?"

"Just that we want to keep it historically accurate." Alice glanced at the reception nurse as if to hint that it might be a good time for an interruption now, but Lola just stood there and watched.

"People in town, not to mention the church, are *not* going to like this," warned Florence. "Mark my word, Alice Howard, you haven't heard the end of this yet."

"No, I figured I hadn't."

Florence smiled that odd little smile that never seemed to engage her eyes. "I just thought that I should let you know about my concerns in person, Alice. It seemed the Christian thing to do."

"I appreciate your taking the time."

Alice tried not to fume as she drove home. She reminded herself that Jesus had said to "love your enemies." Not that Florence was her enemy exactly, but with friends like that. . . . Alice also remembered that Jesus had said to "pray for those who persecuted you." That seemed to fit too. So as she drove, she prayed. "Dear heavenly Father, please help me to be patient with those who don't understand what we're trying to accomplish with our little inn. Teach me to be more loving and kind toward people like Florence." She pressed her lips together, then finally said, "And please bless Florence and show her how much You love her. Amen." Alice sighed. It wasn't always easy to do as the Bible instructed, but in the end it was always worth the effort.

Over the years, she had grown used to being involved in the little flaps that regularly occurred in their church. They were usually other people's problems, and she would come alongside them as the peacemaker. She wasn't accustomed to being an actual part of the problem, and she found it incredibly stressful. Sometimes she wondered if this business of creating an inn would really be worth it in the long run. Then she remembered the fun just yesterday when she and her sisters stripped away layer upon layer of wallpaper. It was like a family history lesson. They had laughed and joked and shared hot peppermint cocoa and all gone to bed tired and happy. Today she simply felt tired. Even though she had gone to part-time at the hospital, it seemed that her days were fuller than ever before. She wondered if it was realistic to keep up this pace indefinitely. The idea of giving up the security of her job, or even an early retirement, worried her even more. The truth was, it still bothered her to have switched over to part-time. What if some sort of financial emergency arose?

She parked in front of the house and stepped out to see the progress. They had started the actual painting three days ago, but it was just starting to look as if they were getting somewhere. She knew the late afternoon light wasn't the best time to view the new color, but just the same she thought she liked it. It really had a warm, cozy, inviting feel, sort of like a cup of cocoa on a cold winter night. And now that Jane was getting some of the lower pieces of trim painted, it seemed to come to life even more.

"What do you think?" called Jane as she climbed down

from a six-foot ladder and wiped her hands on a rag that was tied to her overalls. Jane wore a big smile and a red bandana to hold back her dark hair.

"I like it," said Alice.

"Really?" Jane looked hopeful. "That hasn't exactly been the consensus around here, you know."

"I know. Florence just paid me a visit at the hospital."

"You're kidding! She actually went to your workplace? That woman has some nerve."

"She was already there visiting her great-nephew."

"Yeah, I'll bet she just *happened* to be there too. Just like she just *happened* to be driving by here this morning, and the next thing you know she's standing on the sidewalk throwing one of her 'I'm going to call an emergency board meeting' sort of flips."

"Hi, girls." Louise stepped out onto the porch wearing Jane's apron. "Did Jane tell you that I'm on KP tonight?"

"Yeah, since I'm doing hard labor, it seemed only fair that Louise should cook."

Alice nodded, but wondered, *fair to whom?*

"You look tired, Alice," said Louise. "Long day?"

Alice shrugged.

"Aren't you glad you switched over to part-time?" asked Jane.

"I guess so."

"Well, I'm sure glad you did, Alice." Jane grabbed her hand. "It's more fun when you're around here."

"Fun?" Alice peered curiously at her younger sister. "Are you just looking for another willing worker?"

"Working on the house *is* fun." Jane held her chin up. "I love watching it get fixed up and painted. Honestly, I think that's great fun."

Alice nodded. "Yes, so do I."

"So are you glad about it now?"

"About working on the house?"

"No, silly. About going part-time."

"I think so, but it just takes some getting used to."

"Dinner is almost ready," announced Louise. "Tonight we're having my special corn chowder."

Alice nodded, hoping her face looked more enthusiastic than she felt. She had tasted Louise's "special corn chowder" more times than she cared to remember.

"Is this the same corn chowder you used to make when we were kids?" asked Jane as Louise headed back into the house.

"That's right," called Louise over her shoulder.

Jane poked Alice in the arm. "Maybe you can distract Louise by asking to see the fresh paint in her bedroom while I try to doctor up the soup a bit."

"Seriously?"

"Hey, it's worth a shot. I, for one, happen to be hungry tonight."

Alice grinned. "I'm in."

To Alice's pleased surprise, the corn chowder wasn't half bad. In fact, she even had seconds. Louise kept taking little bites and tasting them with puckered lips, as if something was slightly amiss.

"Louise, is something wrong with your chowder?" asked Jane, suppressing a smile.

"It just tastes different, somehow, but I can't quite put my finger on it."

"Well, I think it's the best you've ever made," said Alice, honestly.

Louise smiled. "Really? Well, thank you, dear. I always did pride myself on my corn chowder. It's a recipe that's been in our family for years. Aunt Ethel gave it to me when I was still a teenager."

"Oh, that figures," said Jane, turning to wink at Alice. "So what did you think of Louise's bedroom color, Alice?"

Alice tried to think of something positive to say about the stark walls now trimmed in a pale shade of green paint that reminded her of the operating room scrub uniforms. "Well, it looked very clean and bright, and nicely done."

"Oh, it'll look much better when we get the wallpaper up

and my things are put into place," said Louise. "Right now it's just a blank slate, but I'll make it my own before long."

By the end of the following week, Alice felt as if she had been pulled in a dozen different directions. Two of the nurses on her staff were caught in a squabble over a private matter that seemed irresolvable to Alice. She was afraid she would have to let one of them go but couldn't decide whether to keep the one who seemed the least to blame or the one who was a better nurse. She hated making decisions like this. On top of that, she had been getting phone calls and visits at work from people like Florence and Lloyd and even Aunt Ethel. On the home front, she was constantly finding herself caught in the middle between her two sisters' tastes in paint colors, wallpapers and basically every single element found in interior design.

"I think we should allow the house to breathe a little," Jane would insist. "Clear some of the junk out and let it be more contemporary."

"You're trying to compromise its historical integrity," Louise would declare. "This is, after all, a Victorian era house. It should be filled with Victorian era furnishings." On they would go for what seemed like hours.

Fortunately, Alice had discovered only today that the county historical committee was more concerned with the exterior of the house than with the interior.

"Alice Howard?" said the woman on the other end of the phone. "I don't know if we've met since I'm fairly new in the area. My name is Irene Watts, and I'm on the county historic preservation committee." She cleared her throat, and Alice braced herself. "There have been numerous complaints in regard to your choice of exterior paint colors."

"Why are you calling me at work?" asked Alice.

"Well, I stopped by your house earlier today, and your two sisters were . . . shall I say, involved in a lively discussion about wallpaper choices. I attempted to broach the exterior paint subject with them, but the older one—Louise, is it?"

"Yes."

"Louise seemed more interested in pinning me down on the necessity of maintaining the historical accuracy in the interior."

"I see." Alice sighed.

"When I informed both of them that the historical society has no intention of playing Big Brother when it comes to a home's interior, your other sister seemed to feel that this was her green light to turn the house into something more modern. I just want to make it perfectly clear that it's only the exterior colors and outside renovations that concern us."

"Thank you, that's good to know. So you're saying we can do as please with the interior?"

"Well, as long as you don't do something terribly radical or extreme. We wouldn't want to see the historical integrity compromised."

"How would you define radical or extreme?"

"For instance we wouldn't like to see you putting in a bowling alley or movie theater." She laughed. "Although I must admit that those things have been done in some cases without creating any problems. But whether you use modern furnishings or antiques is of absolutely no interest to our group."

"Oh."

"I think I simply caught your sisters at an awkward moment," explained Irene in a softer tone. "I ran into Lloyd Tynan at the Coffee Shop—he's an old friend. Anyway, he suggested I might try calling the hospital and directing my concerns to you. He seemed to think you'd be a good mediator."

"I see."

"Anyway, my main question is this: What was your reasoning for choosing those particular exterior colors?"

Alice barely mentioned the name of the firm of color experts before she was interrupted.

"You're kidding? How did you hear about them?"

"My sister knew about them. She's from San Francisco and—"

"Well, she's one smart lady."

"So, are we okay then, on the exterior colors?" Alice asked.

"Of course. You've done it just right. I must say that I personally like the colors a lot, and I was interested in how you managed to come up with something that seemed so historically appropriate, but I had no idea that you'd gone to such trouble. People like you make our jobs so much easier."

"What about the flak I've heard that the townsfolk have been giving your committee?" Alice sighed. "And us."

"Oh, I've seen all this before. Especially in small towns like Acorn Hill, but, trust me, people will get used to it in time."

"In time."

"If it makes you feel any better, I'll try to spread the word around that your house is A-OK with me and the historical society."

"Thanks so much. We'd appreciate that."

"If you have any questions, please, feel free to call. I left my card with your sisters."

"Great. We'll be sure to do that."

"I don't want to make you feel paranoid, but I'd love to check in from time to time, just to see your progress. It's such a beautiful home, so much potential."

"Of course, stop by anytime you like. My sisters will be calmer the next time you visit, I hope. They're both very nice women—under normal circumstances."

Irene laughed. "I'm sure they are. Believe me, I understand how large renovations like this can bring the worst out in people. I've seen marriages literally destroyed over remodeling projects."

"I hope we'll all still be friends when we're finished."

"I'm sure you will."

After Alice hung up, she felt as if she'd made a new, and possibly valuable, friend. She couldn't wait to tell Jane and Louise the good news. Well, that and to warn them to mind their manners a little better when visitors came calling. She feared that Irene was right, perhaps the stress was getting to all of them, or maybe this was just God's way of confirming to her that she had made the right decision to go part-time in her work after all.

Alice prayed that God would continue to lead and guide her as she drove toward home that evening. Then she reminded herself that the best things in life didn't come easily, and that was most likely going to be the case with Grace Chapel Inn. Perhaps she and her sisters were like the children of Israel being led from Egypt to the Promised Land. Hadn't there been a lot of bickering and complaining along the way? She hoped that the three of them wouldn't do anything drastic enough to get themselves stuck in the wilderness. She didn't really think that any of them, well, perhaps excepting Jane, would still be around in forty years.

Chapter Fifteen

Alice arrived home to find Jane and Louise at something of a standoff. From the partially opened door, Louise appeared to be cloistered in her bedroom, surrounded by a number of crates. Jane was clanking around in the kitchen, apparently reorganizing, but Alice felt there was an inordinate amount of banging pots and slamming drawers going on. One thing seemed clear, neither of them appeared willing to talk just now. Certainly not to one another, and they didn't offer much more than a slightly disgruntled greeting to Alice.

Alice felt bewildered by her sisters' behavior and not quite comfortable in her own house. For the first time in ages, she found herself knocking on Aunt Ethel's door.

"Hello, dear," said Aunt Ethel, peering over Alice's shoulder with curiosity. "What brings you over here?"

"Oh, I don't know." Alice sighed and then held up her hands in a somewhat hopeless gesture.

"Well, do come in, dear." Aunt Ethel held the door open wide. "It's chilly out there tonight."

Without waiting for an invitation to sit, Alice flopped

down onto her aunt's overstuffed velvet couch. "I thought maybe you might know what's going on."

"Oh, are Jane and Louise still feuding?"

Alice nodded.

Aunt Ethel snickered slightly as she lowered herself into a padded rocker. "*Those two.*"

"They're both so upset that neither one of them will speak—not even to me. I just don't get it."

"Well, I happened to pop in over there earlier today and I suddenly found myself caught in the middle of their little disagreement."

"I'm guessing it was about the wallpaper." Alice shook her head in disbelief.

"The wallpaper, the paint colors, you name it and those two don't agree on it." Aunt Ethel wore her *I-told-you-so* expression as she contentedly folded her hands in her lap and rocked back and forth.

"I don't see why they won't at least talk to me. It doesn't seem fair that they should shut me out."

Aunt Ethel cleared her throat and then patted her hair. "Well, maybe it has to do with what I told them earlier."

Alice groaned. "Oh, no, what did you tell them, Aunt Ethel?"

"Just that it wasn't fair to constantly stick you in the middle." She leaned forward and peered at Alice. "I told them that I think that it's been taking a toll on you and that they should learn how to settle their petty differences without endlessly putting you into the thick of it. It's just not right!"

"I don't mind really. I'd rather be in the middle of it than on the outside while they both fuss and fume."

"They are grown women and should be able to resolve these little spats on their own. You're a busy woman, Alice. You have your job and your church responsibilities. You certainly can't be expected to play nursemaid to two overgrown—"

"Aunt Ethel, I appreciate your concern for me. I really do." For the second time today, Alice felt tears filling her eyes. "You're not wrong either. It *has* been a little stressful lately."

Her aunt nodded with satisfaction.

"I'm sure that it's helping me to appreciate that I decided to work fewer hours."

"You're certain that's what you wanted to do, dear?"

"I am now."

"I know how you've always loved your job, Alice."

Alice nodded. "I still do, but I'm equally excited about working in the inn."

"But I'm sure you wouldn't want to give up your nursing career completely, Alice. You're so good at it."

Alice smiled. "Thanks, Aunt Ethel. That's probably one of the nicest things you've ever said to me, and you're right.

I'm not ready to give it up just yet. I know that it'll be time for me to retire someday."

"Well, it's true, dear. You are a natural-born nurse. You've always been good at taking care of others, but sometimes I expect you need someone to look after you. Now how about a nice cup of tea?" She pushed herself to her feet. "I guess I almost forgot my manners."

Alice ended up eating a small, simple dinner of cinnamon toast and peaches with her aunt. When it was all said and done, she decided that this was probably one of her best diplomatic efforts so far—not that she had intended it for such. By the time she was ready to go back home, Aunt Ethel took her by the hand and smiled.

"Now, don't you worry about a thing, Alice. I'm sure that everything will turn out just fine for your little inn. Remember, it's often the best things in life that seem the hardest to come by."

Alice nodded. "You know, I was thinking that same thing as I drove home from work tonight."

The house was quiet when Alice slipped back inside. She paused to look at the bare walls in the dining and living rooms. Completely stripped of their many layers of wallpaper, at first they looked cold and naked, but after a while she thought they looked pretty, all clean and bare like that—as if you could see the real lines and architectural structure of the house. She noticed the interesting wood trim around doors and windows and the crown molding around the high ceilings, as if seeing these things for the first time. It really was a lovely old home. It just needed a little tender loving care, not to mention elbow grease, to bring it back into its prime.

She quietly tiptoed up the staircase toward her room. Strips of yellow light were coming from beneath both her sisters' doors. *Well, they haven't murdered each other yet*, she thought. It wasn't long before she had on her cozy flannel pajamas, the comforting ones with little teapots and teacups printed on the fabric, as well as the hand-knitted wool slippers that Louise had sent her last Christmas. She had just picked up her new mystery book when she heard a little tap-tap-tap on her door.

She cracked the door open to see Jane wearing a dark red chenille throw like a shawl over her pale lavender flannel nightgown. Jane's thin bare feet looked cold and pale standing on the hardwood floor. Alice opened the door wider and motioned her forlorn-looking younger sister to come in.

"Want to talk?" asked Alice.

Jane nodded.

"I feel absolutely rotten," Jane confessed as she sank into Alice's easy chair by the window. She wrapped her throw more tightly around her shoulders and tucked her bare feet up under the hem of her gown. "I've acted like a complete moron today. I'm sure Louise will never speak to me again. She's probably in there packing her bags right now. I've heard her making all sorts of shuffling noises. I'm so sorry, Alice. I'm sure I've ruined the whole idea of running an inn for everyone."

"Oh, Jane." Alice shook her head. "You're overreacting. I suspect Louise is just unpacking her crates, making herself more at home. Oh, she may have gotten her feelings hurt a bit today, but then you know that our Louise is like a rock. She doesn't budge that easily."

Jane rolled her eyes. "You're telling me."

"I heard you two had a bad day."

"Does the whole town know?"

"It's possible."

Jane moaned.

"First I heard it from Irene—"

"That historical society lady?" Jane frowned.

"She's actually pretty nice."

"*Humph.*"

"And then from Aunt Ethel."

"Well, that figures."

"What happened?"

"You know. Just the same ol' same ol'."

Just then a sharper knock-knock interrupted their conversation. "Come in, Louise," called Alice without even getting up.

"Oh!" Louise looked surprised to see Jane. "Am I interrupting something?"

Alice patted the bed beside her and smiled. "No, I think you should probably join us."

Louise adjusted her dressing gown more neatly around her and then sat at the edge of the bed next to Alice. Her lips were pressed firmly together, but her eyes looked tired and sad.

"I know you girls had a bad day today," said Alice. "Let's just say I heard it through the grapevine, Louise."

"That nosy historical lady," said Jane.

"Figures," said Louise.

"Now, listen, you two. Irene is really quite nice and reasonable. Of course, she thinks you two are both certifiably nuts. She wants you to understand that the society doesn't give a hoot what you do with the interior of our house—"

"But what about—"

"Louise," warned Alice. "I'm not finished. Anyway, Irene was very pleased to find out how we discovered the original paint colors for the exterior. She happens to like them too. She said she is going to try to spread the word around that we are historically correct."

"H.C.?" Jane said with a smirk.

"I guess you could call it that." Alice nodded. "I also had a nice little chat with Aunt Ethel tonight. She mentioned that you two got a bit out of hand too, although she didn't seem surprised."

"Yes, she made that perfectly clear," said Louise as she played with the belt to her robe. "I'm sure that it's exactly what she expected."

"I wanted to tell you both something." Alice waited to make sure she had her sisters' attention. They both looked up expectantly.

"Oh dear, is it bad?" asked Louise with worried eyes.

"Are you ready to bail on us now?" asked Jane.

Alice firmly shook her head. "No. I just wanted to let you know that I'm really glad that I went to part-time at work. I know I was worried about it the other day. And I'm sure I haven't quite been myself lately, but now I know for absolute certain that it was the right thing to do."

Jane smiled. "I'm so relieved. I was feeling guilty, thinking that maybe I'd talked you into something you weren't really happy about. And then you've got Louise and me at home, waiting for you like a couple of spoiled children who need a referee to get along."

Louise shook her head. "Goodness, Alice, I wouldn't blame you if you'd decided you wanted to go back to working full time just to avoid us. We've behaved miserably."

"I apologize," said Jane. "To both of you. I hope you'll forgive me."

"I'm sorry too," admitted Louise. "I'm not usually like this. I think it has something to do with being back at home again, especially after all these years. It's as if I'm suddenly seventeen again, trying to play the mothering role and thinking I can make my two younger sisters just fall into step." She shook her head. "It's really rather silly."

Jane got up and sat down on the bed next to Alice now. She took Alice's hand in hers. "Oh, it feels so much more balanced and peaceful having you here."

Louise reached over and patted Alice on the back. "Yes, dear, you have no idea how much we need your help around here."

Alice chuckled. "Oh yes, I think I do."

It didn't take long for Alice to adjust to her new role at the hospital. She let the administrator deal with the two nurses who couldn't get along. After a week or so, she was getting better at accepting the fact that she didn't need to take responsibility for everything that happened there anymore.

"You need to learn to let go and let God," Vera reminded her during their morning walk one day. "You have such a tendency to carry the world on your shoulders, Alice."

"I know." Alice zipped her sweatshirt up higher against the chilly morning air.

"Old habits are hard to break. It just seems that most of

my life I've been taking care of people. It just seems natural to think that everything is up to me to work out or resolve or fix up somehow."

Vera laughed. "Well, thank the good Lord that it's not."

Alice nodded. "Yeah, if it were, we'd be in some kind of a mess."

"It's okay to let people help you out too, Alice. You know, that's why God put us all down here together."

Alice turned and smiled at her friend. "Thanks for reminding me."

"Well, we all need a little reminder from time to time."

Chapter Sixteen

During the week after the little standoff, Jane and Louise both worked at more civilized behavior, but it was plain to see that their differences in style and décor were deeply ingrained into the fiber of their personalities. Alice wasn't really surprised by this. She still remembered how these traits had displayed themselves throughout her sisters' childhoods.

Jane, the perennial tomboy, adventure seeker, free-spirited artist, had grown up in the sixties and had always leaned heavily toward no-nonsense contemporary styles. She still loved bold colors and sweeping statements, clean-lined furnishings and large striking pieces of modern art. It's just who she was.

Louise, on the other hand, had always been a very feminine girl. She had been a teenager in the fifties and had enjoyed wearing pastels and ruffles. She had never liked to get her hands dirty and nothing pleased her more than playing the piano in a frilly dress with a nearby vase of tea roses perfectly centered on a lace doily.

So it was only natural that Louise was drawn to floral wallpapers and fussy curtains. She loved anything with flowers or lace.

Fortunately, during the past week, instead of fussing over the interior design decisions, Jane and Louise had managed to distract themselves with the mundane tasks that no one could disagree on. All sorts of jobs needed to be done, things like sanding the wood molding and prepping the walls. Jane had even managed to talk Louise into donning a pair of coveralls and gloves and sanding the staircase hand railing one afternoon.

"It wasn't so bad," confessed Louise that night at dinner. "I wore safety goggles and one of those fiber masks, and then I simply paced myself."

"She did a good job," admitted Jane.

"I can't wait to put on a pair of coveralls tomorrow," said Alice. "I feel like I've been missing out on all the fun."

Louise shook her head. "Fun might be a bit of an overstatement, Alice."

Jane winked at her as she ladled out another serving of black bean soup and then topped it with a generous dollop of sour cream.

By the end of the following day, Alice could tell that both her sisters' patience was starting to wear thin again. Not only that, but they were also quickly approaching the time when more decisions had to be made. Louise had already been poking around in the attic and bringing down old pieces of Victorian furniture that she thought would look perfect in the guest rooms. Meanwhile, Jane kept hinting that Louise's flowery wallpaper selections would only make the house look too fussy and that the walls would look much better painted in some bold and interesting colors. Alice felt like a Ping-Pong ball bouncing back and forth between her two sisters. She honestly wanted to encourage both of them and somehow to manage to make everyone happy, yet she felt unsure about how they would find a happy compromise.

By mid-morning on a particularly controversial Saturday—her two sisters were grumbling about wallpaper again—Alice decided she definitely needed a break. She figured it was only a matter of time before Jane and Louise got into a really serious disagreement that even Alice wouldn't be able to referee. Louise had already taken numerous Victorian replica wallpaper books and spread them across the dining room table like an out-of-control flower garden. Then she had cornered Alice and demanded an opinion regarding the blue and pink "Posy Rosy" and the yellow and purple "Lacy Lilac" wallpapers. "For the foyer," Louise urged her. "Don't you think the Posy Rosy would be perfectly warm and inviting?"

"I'm not terribly fond of pink and blue," Alice admitted.

"Then how about the Lacy Lilac?"

"For the dining room?" Alice asked weakly.

Louise nodded. "Yes, I think it will really brighten it up in here."

"I'm just not sure." Alice squinted her eyes and tried to imagine their dining room walls covered with flowers. For one thing, she knew Jane would throw a fit. She'd already made it clear that she wanted the kitchen and dining area to be a little more contemporary. And this seemed fair since Jane was to be the main cook.

"We *must* make a decision," said Louise. "It will take two to four weeks for the wallpapers to arrive."

"Wallpapers?" echoed Jane from the front foyer. "Did I hear someone mention wallpaper again?"

"I need to go to town," Alice said as she quickly made her way to the back porch, where she removed her coveralls and left them on a shelf. She could hear her sisters' voices growing louder as she cut through the backyard, passed Aunt Ethel's and headed toward town.

She stopped in the Coffee Shop and ordered a cup of tea.

"No pie today?" asked Hope.

Alice shook her head. "I'm trying to cut back on the sweets."

Hope nodded. "Yeah, I know what you mean. We gotta watch our girlish figures."

Alice laughed.

"So how's it going up at the house?"

"Don't ask."

"That bad, huh?" Hope leaned over as if to get the real scoop. "Your sisters driving you nuts again?"

Alice blinked in surprise. "How—I mean, what makes you think that?"

Hope grinned. "Word gets around."

"Well, it's awfully hard to make decisions about things like paint colors and wallpaper."

"Hey, I walked by your house yesterday and I happen to think your exterior paint colors look great."

"You and about four other people in town."

"Still catching some flak, are you?"

Alice sighed. "I'm sure we won't hear the end of it for a long, long time."

"Didn't Irene's article in the newspaper help?" Hope refilled a coffee cup at the other end of the counter. "I found it pretty interesting myself. I didn't realize there was so much to know about historic colors."

"That was a nice article." Alice sipped her tea. "And I hope it will help convince some people in this town that Victorian homes were originally painted something other than white or peach."

"I heard Mabel Torrence saying that she might just go

ahead and paint her house pink now. Said she always fancied a nice flamingo shade of pink, but that Harold would never agree to it when he was alive." Hope chuckled. "Might make the poor old guy roll over in his grave though."

"Flamingo pink?" Alice tried to imagine the little pale gray bungalow painted a shade of bright pink and shuddered. "Goodness, I hope we haven't started something that—"

"Oh, don't worry." Hope waved her hand. "This town could use a little more color."

Alice finished her tea and went across the street to the bookstore. She figured she could spend a few more minutes just looking around before she forced herself to head back home and face the fray.

"How's it going, Alice?" asked Viola.

"Okay, I guess."

"You don't sound too sure."

Alice forced a smile. "Well, we're just reaching the stage where it's time to make some decisions on the interior of the house."

Viola grinned. "I'll bet your two sisters are probably going at it all over again."

Alice shrugged. "Seems everyone knows about our troubles."

"It's a small town, Alice."

"So I've heard."

"I've never seen two sisters less alike than Jane and Louise." Viola lowered her voice a little since there was another customer in the shop. "I like Louise just fine. Why, she and I even share the same interest in nineteenth-century literature. But Jane, she's a bit too outspoken if you ask me."

"Oh, you haven't had a good chance to get acquainted with Jane yet. She's a very creative person, very talented. In fact, she's a free thinker, sort of like you. You should get to know her better."

"I'm sure you're right. My first impressions are often a little off."

Alice glanced around the bookstore. "Say, Viola, you wouldn't have anything on home décor in here, would you?"

"Well, now that you mention it, I just got some books in the other day, and come to think of it, I might have one that's right up your alley. Let's see, where did I put those?"

Finally Viola emerged from the backroom with a large book in her hands. "Here it is." She held up the book *Simply Victorian.*

Alice took the book from her and began to flip through the glossy pages. It was a pretty book, full of nice color photos, but what Alice immediately noticed was that the rooms didn't appear overly fussy and frilly. "This is different."

"That's what I thought too. If you read the introduction,

it explains that it's the Victorian style simplified. I think it's rather nice myself. Maybe it will be of some help to you and your sisters."

Alice nodded. "Yes, this might be just the ticket." She gladly paid for the expensive book and then hurried home.

She was barely in the front door when she heard Jane's voice from the dining room. "Oh, Louise, how on earth do you expect me to serve food in a room that looks like a bedroom?"

"A bedroom?" Louise's voice was a bit sharp. "What do you mean—"

"Hello?" called Alice in a tentative voice.

"Alice," Louise turned to her with a slightly flushed face. "I'm so glad that you're back. Our little sister doesn't like these authentic Victorian reproduction wallpapers."

"I think you two need a timeout," said Alice with a weak smile.

"We *need* to make some decisions," said Louise. "This wallpaper can take up to four weeks for delivery, and that's with a rush order and we've got to—"

"Why do we have to have wallpaper in the first place?" Jane closed the wallpaper book with a thud. Wendell, who had been lying under the dining table, got up quickly and left the room.

Smart cat, thought Alice.

Louise patted Jane on the head. "Settle down, little sister."

Jane sighed. "Yeah, I guess I am getting fairly worked up. Sorry."

"Okay, can you both give me your attention for just one minute?" pleaded Alice as she opened her bag. "Viola showed me this great book at Nine Lives, and it might be just the answer." She pulled out the large book and set it on top of the wallpaper books that were spread across the dining room table.

"*Simply Victorian,*" Jane read in a suspicious tone.

"Let's have a look," said Louise.

"Hey, that's not half bad," said Jane as they studied a two-page photo of a Victorian dining room.

"See," said Alice. "It's not all flowers and frills and yet it still looks nice."

"No wallpaper," noted Louise with a slight frown.

"It doesn't need it," said Jane. "See how the architecture and wood paneling really stand out against that pale blue paint. It's lovely."

"The furniture is antique," said Alice, "but it doesn't look too busy or crowded."

"Or fussy," added Jane.

They flipped through some more pages, and before

long it seemed that Louise and Jane were coming to a real place of compromise.

"I guess I could give up some of the fussiness," admitted Louise.

"And I suppose it would look silly to have everything all modern and contemporary in here," said Jane. "Just the same I'd like it to feel clean and light and cheerful."

"That's what I want too," said Louise.

"Then maybe we're all in agreement." Alice smiled hopefully.

"I think we're getting closer." Jane pointed out a photo with a shining mahogany table with a beautiful bouquet of fresh flowers in a crystal vase on top. "Now, I think that's simply gorgeous. I would love to grow our own flowers and have arrangements like that throughout the house." She turned to Louise. "Really, isn't that much better than silk flowers and frilly doilies?"

Louise nodded. "Yes, I think I might have to agree with you on that."

"So what do you think of that color for our dining room?" asked Alice as she pointed to the background color in that particular photo.

"It's kind of a celery green," observed Jane. "I like it."

"I like it too," said Louise, "but do you think it would look right in here?"

"I think it would be lovely," said Jane. "Fresh and clean, and a nice contrast with the dark wood dining room furniture. Can't you just see it with a bouquet like that on the table?"

"I can!" Alice felt excited now.

"It looks to me like a faux finish," said Jane as she bent over to examine the photo more carefully.

"What's that?" asked Alice.

"It's when you use several shades of paint and a special technique. It's easier to show you than to explain it." Jane stood up straight and rubbed her hands together. "When do we begin?"

Alice shrugged. "It's up to you guys."

"What do you think of that area rug in the picture?" asked Louise in what seemed a slightly cautious voice. "I mean, I realize that Jane has been saying that she doesn't want to see a lot of area rugs strewn all over the place."

"It's actually quite nice," admitted Jane. "Not too busy."

Louise smiled now. "Well, I happen to have a rug almost exactly like that. It's pure wool and just the right size for this room."

"This is great," said Jane.

Alice nodded. "I think we're onto something, girls."

"Too bad we didn't stumble across this book sooner," said Louise. "I'm sure we gave Aunt Ethel something new to talk about today."

"Aunt Ethel was here?" Alice felt her eyebrows going up.

"We were acting like children again," admitted Louise. "I'm sure Aunt Ethel has already told Lloyd and half the town about our little disagreement by now."

"Oh well." Alice sighed. "It's not as if there aren't rumors going around Acorn Hill already."

"We're going to have quite a reputation before long," said Jane with what almost seemed like pride.

"I have an idea," said Louise. "Why don't we all go out for lunch right now? My treat. We'll put on our best manners and show everyone just how much we really love each other."

"Give them something new to talk about?"

They took their paint samples and new décor book to the Coffee Shop and sat around a big corner table. Hope winked at Alice as she refilled their water glasses. "Everything okay here?" she asked.

"Couldn't be better," said Louise.

"What do you think of this color for our dining room?" Alice asked Hope.

"*Ooh*, that's nice."

Before the day was over, they had picked out most of their interior paint colors and had even agreed upon a few samples of some of the less intricate styles of wallpaper. If all went as planned, then the finished appearance of the inn would be fresh and clean and yet elegant.

"I think the colors we've chosen will feel nice and peaceful," Alice said later on that evening as they sat around the kitchen table sipping cinnamon tea. "Our guests will just sigh deeply when they step in the front door. They'll know this is a place where they can simply relax."

"A place where one can be refreshed and encouraged," said Louise.

"A place of hope and healing," added Jane.

"A place where God is at home," said Alice.

"I like that," said Jane. "Maybe we should put those words on a plaque or something."

"I have a special catalog that makes nameplates and such," said Louise as she furiously scribed their words on a page of her notebook. "Shall I order us up a plaque with that on it?"

Jane nodded. "Yes, we can put it right by the front door for everyone who enters. I especially like what Alice said: *A place where God is at home.*"

Alice smiled. "I think Father would love that."

Chapter Seventeen

*O*nce the colors and general direction of the interior design were agreed upon, it became clear that Jane had a natural gift for decorating. This made perfect sense to Alice since Jane had always been the one interested in art, but Louise seemed slightly surprised about what she referred to as "Jane's knack." Soon Jane began making suggestions for rearranging pieces of furniture, or hanging a mirror on a certain wall, or even the careful placement of a potted plant. At first Louise would resist these changes, but she soon realized that Jane knew exactly what she was doing. Before long, both Louise and Alice decided that Jane should take charge of the interior design.

"That doesn't mean you get to make *all* the decisions completely on your own," Louise reminded her. "We all have to agree with anything major."

Jane nodded. "Believe me, I know."

"Not that you've given us anything to disagree with," said Alice. "So far, we love what you've been doing, Jane."

"But I'd still like a say," said Louise.

"I've already thought about what I'd like to do in Mother and Father's room," said Jane. "I was sitting up there this afternoon and got hit with an inspiration. Don't worry, I'll run it by you two first."

"I'm sure it'll be nice," said Alice. "It's so dreary and faded looking now. Father never wanted to change a thing up there."

"I got an idea for the other guest rooms." Jane said this with a twinkle in her eye. "I thought perhaps we could each choose the décor for our old bedrooms. Since we used to live there, we would know them the best. It might sort of give them an individual identity, don't you think?"

"Really?" Louise looked slightly stunned. "You'd actually allow us to pick out our own style of décor in a room, Jane?"

She grinned. "Sure. Who knows, we might even have a guest or two who really wants to stay in a frilly, old-fashioned Victorian bedroom."

"Well, I wouldn't need to make it overly fussy . . ."

"I'd like mine to be more of a country-styled room," said Alice thoughtfully. "Perhaps with a patchwork quilt. Something cheerful and light."

"See," said Jane. "Your input will give the rooms more personality. We should probably give them some sort of names, so we can distinguish them from each other. I was thinking of calling Father and Mother's the Garden Room, since it faces the garden. Father always told me how much Mother loved her flowers."

"What kind of names should we give our rooms?" asked Louise as she set aside her knitting.

"My old bedroom faces east," said Alice. "How about if I call it the Sunrise Room?"

"That's sweet," said Jane.

Louise frowned. "My old room faces north. I don't want to call it the Arctic Room."

"Well, think about some sort of theme that you'd like to have in your room," suggested Jane. "Some color you like, or something you enjoy."

"Music?" said Louise.

Jane nodded. "That's nice, but we might not want to call it the Music Room. That might be confusing."

"How about the Symphony Room?" asked Louise. "I have a beautiful old violin that belonged to Eliot as a boy. I could display it on the wall."

"That sounds lovely," said Alice.

"Now how about your old room, Jane?"

"Hmm, Alice's name gives me an idea. I used to enjoy sitting in my room and watching the sun set. I could call mine the Sunset Room, and that will go nicely with the palette of colors I've decided on."

"I like that," said Alice. "So we have the Garden Room, the Symphony Room, the Sunrise Room, and the Sunset Room."

"That's nice," said Jane.

By the middle of the following week, Alice felt that everything was falling neatly into place. Other than their biggest project, replacing the slate-covered roof, Jim Sharp's renovations seemed to be moving along like clockwork. The exterior painting was nearly halfway completed, and Alice thought it looked quite lovely. Other than an unsolved plumbing problem that left the third floor temporarily without water or bathrooms, life seemed to be running fairly smoothly—that is, until Alice came home one evening to find a man standing in their front yard.

"Hello, I'm Mike Wall," the man said, handing her his card. "Are you one of the owners of this lovely home?"

"Yes. I'm Alice Howard."

"Sorry to just drop by like this, but I heard about your property. As you can see by my card, I'm a real estate developer. My office is in Pittsburgh, but I work throughout the state locating and developing unique properties."

"But I—I don't understand..." Alice studied the middle-aged man carefully. His navy blue suit looked quite expensive and he drove some sort of fancy European sports car.

He smiled, revealing a straight set of perfectly white

teeth. "I'm sorry to catch you by surprise, Alice, but one of your relatives informed me that you might be interested in selling your home."

She blinked. "Do you mean one of my sisters contacted you?"

He nodded. "Yes, something like that."

"But that's impossible. We plan to turn this into—"

"Now, let me assure you that I only make offers on the finest sorts of real estate. I haven't seen the inside of your home yet, but I'm impressed with what's been done on the outside, and I understand there's a bit of land and a carriage house and—"

"But it's *not* for sale," said Alice quickly. "I don't know where you got such an idea—"

"Your sister told a mutual friend, and I thought I'd come out to get a better look." He smiled again. "I'm sure you'll find my offer to be more than fair. I've checked local real estate values in your town, and I can assure you that I'm willing to do much better than what—"

"Hey, Alice," called Jane from the front porch. Alice could tell by the curious expression on Jane's face that she hadn't met this pushy man yet.

"Jane, come and meet Mike Wall," said Alice as her younger sister joined them. "He seems to think that our house is for sale."

"Well, now I knew that you hadn't actually put it on the market yet, but according to your sister—"

"*Our sister?*" Jane glanced at Alice as she pulled her thick cardigan sweater more tightly around her.

He looked uncomfortable. "I don't recall her name. She's older."

"*Louise!*" Jane and Alice exclaimed simultaneously.

He nodded. "Yes, that sounds right. Anyway, according to your sister and my good friend Lloyd Tynan, you ladies might be open to hearing my more than generous offer for your property."

"It's *not* for sale!" declared Jane, much more emphatically than Alice had been able to do. Alice shook her head for additional emphasis.

"Like I told—er—was it Alice?" he asked. "Don't be too quick to turn me away before you hear what I have to offer."

"We don't want to sell our house," said Alice. "This is all some sort of a silly mistake."

"Not according to Lloyd and your sister. They seemed quite certain that you'd be interested in hearing my offer."

"Well, why don't you come into the house," said Jane in a stiff voice. "It's getting quite cold out here."

"Where's Louise?" Alice whispered into Jane's ear as they went up the front porch steps.

"I don't know. She left this afternoon and she's not back yet."

Jane led Mike into the parlor while Alice put away her jacket and purse. She wished that Louise would hurry up and come home, and straighten up this crazy nonsense. Why on earth would Louise and Lloyd Tynan tell this virtual stranger that their house was for sale?

"I realize how folks can get an emotional attachment to a family home," he was saying when Alice joined them. "But you need to keep things in perspective. A place like this can be quite expensive to keep up, and there are taxes—did you know that they'll go up with every improvement? Right now while you've got the house almost fixed up it will have good value, but wait a couple of years and who knows?"

"But we have no intention of selling it." Jane's voice was growing increasingly irate.

"Are all three of you equal owners?" he asked as he opened a little notebook and jotted something down.

"Yes," answered Alice.

"And all equal investors in this renovation?"

Alice glanced at Jane.

"I'm not sure that is any of your business." Jane brushed some dust from the knees of her overalls and then quickly stood up, obviously hinting that it was time for him to leave.

He nodded and closed his notebook. "I see. Perhaps your other sister would think otherwise."

"I'm sure this is just some mistake," said Alice. "We're sorry to have wasted your time."

He stood now. "No problem. When do you expect your other sister will be home?"

"I have absolutely no idea," said Jane as she moved toward the parlor door. Alice was surprised she hadn't simply grabbed the fellow by his designer suit and tossed him out by now.

But he was in no hurry as he handed his business card to Jane now. "I'd like for her to give me a call."

"Fine." Jane nodded briskly. "We'll let her know."

"Okay." He smiled again, directing his charm at Jane with what seemed to be full throttle. "Hey, I really like what you're doing around here. It's a lovely house. Lots of potential. You should be proud."

"Thank you." She had him nearly to the front door now.

"I'll be in touch," he said as Jane shut the door behind him.

"The very nerve of that guy!" Jane turned around to face Alice now. "What in heaven's name is Louise up to, talking to realtors behind our backs? What could she possibly be thinking?"

"We don't know any of this for sure, Jane. Don't start imagining things."

Jane marched toward the kitchen. "Did I imagine that realtor, Alice?"

"No, but it just makes no sense."

"Think about it, it makes perfect sense. Louise has been investing the most capital into our renovation. What if she thinks she has the right to sell out if she wants." Jane shook her head. "It's partially my fault, because I've been so argumentative with her. Who would blame her for wanting out?"

"You don't know that, Jane."

"What if she thinks we can all make a lot of money on the deal? Remember how she said real estate was the best kind of investment. What if she's just playing big sister and thinks this is in our best interest?"

"Louise wouldn't do something like that without discussing it with us first. Don't get yourself all worked up over nothing. I'm sure she has a perfectly logical explanation."

"But it's so—"

"Hello," called Louise from the foyer. "Anybody home?"

"We're in the kitchen," called Jane in a slightly irritated voice.

"What's wrong?" asked Louise as she removed her brown leather gloves.

"You tell us, Louise." Jane peered at her oldest sister.

"What?" Louise took off her long camel coat and laid it

across the back of the chair and stared at her sisters. "What on earth is going on here?"

"That's what we want to know." Jane set a pot onto the stovetop. "Are you selling out on us, Louise?"

"What are you talking about, Jane?"

"Did you tell that Mike Wall fellow that we were interested in selling our house?" Jane turned and looked at Louise. With her arms folded she waited for her sister's response.

"Mike Wall?" Louise looked to Alice with raised brows as she shook her head. "Who is that?"

"The realtor," explained Alice, fishing in her pocket for his business card. "He wants you to call him."

"A realtor? Why in the world do I want to call a realtor?"

"To sell our house." Jane spoke slowly now, as if Louise wasn't quite listening. "Apparently Mike Wall has some really great offer. He says that you and Lloyd Tynan told him that we might be interested."

"Lloyd Tynan and I?" Louise looked truly stumped now. "Why, I haven't spoken with Lloyd in weeks. Goodness knows, Aunt Ethel would've made it known to everyone if I had."

"*Aunt Ethel,*" Alice said suddenly. "At first Mike Wall said he'd spoken to a *relative*. I guess I just assumed it was one of my sisters, and then when Jane pleaded innocent, we naturally thought—"

Louise looked scandalized. "You actually thought I'd try to sell our house without even discussing it with the two of you?"

"Well, it all happened so quickly," said Jane as she twisted a dish towel in her hands.

"We didn't know what to think," offered Alice. "I'm so sorry, Louise."

She sniffed. "I thought you knew me better than that."

Jane put her arm around Louise's shoulders. "Oh, Louise, it's all my fault. I'm so sorry. Alice told me you would never do something like that. I don't know why I didn't believe her. That presumptuous realtor, well, he just got me all fired up. Please, forgive me, Louise—me and my big mouth."

"It's all right, Jane. Under the circumstances, I might've done the same."

"But I should've known better." Jane shook her head. "To be honest, I haven't had the best day anyway. I spilt a whole gallon of paint in the Sunrise Room this afternoon." She glanced at Alice nervously. "Sorry. But, don't worry, I have an idea for doing a pickle finish on the floor anyway, and I think it will go nicely with the country theme you're planning in there."

"It's okay," Alice reassured her. "But back to this realtor. I wonder if he spoke to Aunt Ethel and then simply assumed she was our sister. He did say *older* sister."

Louise smiled slyly. "*Older* sister? Well, of course, it *must* be Aunt Ethel. She must've been talking to Lloyd. But what gives her the right to put our house on the market?"

"Well, it's not exactly *on* the market," said Alice.

"You wouldn't have known that after listening to that fast-talking realtor." Jane made a face. "Talk about slick."

"He mentioned something about a possible development of the whole property," said Alice. "Even the carriage house. Do you suppose that Aunt Ethel wants to move?"

"I wonder if she needs money," said Jane.

"But the carriage house belongs to the family property," said Louise. "My understanding was that Father only gave it to her to live in, for the course of her lifetime, but that it wasn't hers to sell."

"That's right." Alice sat down in a chair and leaned her elbows onto the table.

Louise frowned. "I don't know why she'd do something like this."

"We don't know for sure that she did," said Alice.

"I think we should get to the bottom of this," said Jane, "and the sooner the better."

They marched right over to Aunt Ethel's little house and knocked on the door. When no one answered, Alice remembered that Aunt Ethel liked to join Lloyd for Bingo Night on Thursdays.

"It's at Town Hall," she explained. "They serve chili dogs at five o'clock. Aunt Ethel likes to help out in the kitchen and calling numbers. It's sponsored by the Chamber, and they raise money for the elementary school."

"That's right," said Louise. "She invited me to go with her when I first came home, but that was back before the situation with Lloyd Tynan got out of hand. She hasn't invited me since."

Jane laughed. "I can just see you playing bingo at Town Hall. Yeah, and eating a chili dog with onions to boot!"

Louise involuntarily brushed off an imaginary crumb from her mauve cashmere sweater. "That would be something now, wouldn't it?"

Alice sighed. "Well, unless we want to storm Town Hall and make a complete spectacle of ourselves tonight, I guess we'll just have to wait until later."

"At least we have a pretty good idea that it *was* Aunt Ethel," said Jane. "That's something of a relief."

Alice wasn't so sure. Why would Aunt Ethel pull something like this in the first place? Perhaps even more perplexing was that Alice had come to feel as if she and Aunt Ethel had actually become a little closer after that last visit when her aunt had seemed so supportive of the development of the inn. But then, if Alice knew anything about her aunt, she knew that you could never completely count on that woman.

Father used to say that one of Aunt Ethel's most charming personality traits was her complete unpredictability.

"My little sister is just like the weather," he would say with a knowing but loving smile.

But Alice knew that some forms of weather could be damaging and destructive. And she sincerely hoped that Aunt Ethel wasn't as responsible for this little storm as it appeared. Otherwise, they might as well start calling their aunt "Hurricane Ethel."

Chapter Eighteen

They decided to wait until after breakfast before invading their aunt's little cottage the following morning. Fortunately it was Alice's day off. Not that she particularly enjoyed controversy or even wanted to see Aunt Ethel confronted like this. Mostly she wanted to see the truth brought to light as well as help make sure that no feelings got irreparably hurt.

"Goodness," said Aunt Ethel when she opened the door to see her three nieces standing on her little porch. She looked as if she had only just gotten up. She was still wearing her purple bathrobe, which proved a striking contrast against her flame red hair that had yet to be combed and tamed. "To what do I owe this unexpected visit?"

"May we come in?" asked Louise in a firm tone.

"Well, certainly." Aunt Ethel held the door open and stepped back. "Is something wrong?"

"Possibly," said Jane.

"Why don't you sit down at the table," offered Aunt Ethel. "I'll put the tea kettle on, and we can visit."

"That's okay, we don't need any tea," said Jane. "Just some answers."

"Well, all right then." Aunt Ethel led them to the kitchen, sat down at the table and waited, glancing nervously at Alice as if hoping for some sort of potential backup. Alice nodded but kept her mouth closed.

Louise cleared her throat as she placed her hands on the table. Jane and Alice had chosen her as the designated speaker. They both knew that Louise could be both tactful and firm. "We had a visit from a man named Mike Wall yesterday, Aunt Ethel." She waited for any reaction from her aunt.

"Mike Wall?" Aunt Ethel firmly shook her head, jostling her chins. "Don't recall that name. Now what's this to do with me?"

"Mike Wall is a real-estate developer. A friend of Lloyd's."

Aunt Ethel's eyes flickered a bit. "Oh, maybe that's that Michael fellow. Nice looking young man, drives a fancy car."

"That sounds like him," said Alice.

"His father is a good friend of Lloyd's. Michael was in town the other day, and Lloyd introduced him to me at the Coffee Shop."

"And?" Louise waited.

"And what?"

"Did you mention our house being available for sale?" Louise peered at Aunt Ethel.

"Goodness me, of course not." Aunt Ethel sat up straighter and patted her hair.

"Did you mention our house at all?"

"Well, now, I suppose I may have. Simply in passing."

"What exactly did you say about our house?" asked Louise.

"Just that you girls were renovating it . . ." Aunt Ethel smiled a bit sheepishly now. "And that perhaps it was getting to be too much for you—"

"Too much for us?" Jane's brows lifted.

"Jane," Louise gently patted her arm. "Remember."

"Sorry." Jane looked down at the table.

"What exactly did you mean, Aunt Ethel," continued Louise, "when you told Mike Wall that our house was getting to be too much for us?"

Aunt Ethel fluttered her hands. "Oh, nothing really. I simply might have mentioned that you sisters were squabbling over the renovations and that perhaps it would be better for everyone concerned if the family home was sold."

"So you gave Mike Wall the impression that we were interested in selling?"

"I suppose I may have."

"And you were going to include the carriage house in this little real estate transaction too?"

Aunt Ethel just shook her head. "Well, no, of course not."

"That's not what Mike thinks. He seemed to assume the entire property is up for sale."

"Well, I suppose he could've gotten that impression. I did mention that the lot was fairly large, with some good potential. I was just talking. He'd been telling Lloyd and me about how he locates these unique properties, many of them historic, and he develops them and then sells them for a tidy little profit." Her eyes grew wide. "Did you know that he paid close to a million dollars for a property that didn't sound much better than your place. Although it did have more land and—"

"Aunt Ethel," said Louise, "the house isn't yours to sell."

"Well, I know that." Aunt Ethel stood now, crossing her arms across her chest with a frown. "I was only trying to help you girls out. Goodness, if someone were going to offer me a large chunk of money for a piece of property I owned, I'd be nothing but grateful."

"You know that we're turning the house into a bed and breakfast," said Jane.

Aunt Ethel rolled her eyes. "Well, so you say, but I happen to think that bed and breakfast idea is still a long shot. Lloyd said that your business license isn't even approved yet. And your renovations are still—"

"Aunt Ethel." Louise stood now. "What you did caused

us some unnecessary problems, and we think it was wrong for you to interfere like that."

Aunt Ethel blinked. "I don't see how you can say that. I was simply trying to be helpful. Mike Wall is willing to pay top dollar for that house—"

"Does this mean that you actually want us to sell our house?" asked Alice, despite her earlier resolve to remain silent. "Do you really want to see some strangers living in our house, or someone developing it into apartments, or something like that?"

"Well, now, I don't know about that."

"Don't you like having us as your neighbors, Aunt Ethel?" asked Jane. "Do you really dislike us that much?"

"Of course not." Now Aunt Ethel began to sniffle. She pulled a tissue out from her robe sleeve and daubed her eyes. "I don't know why you're all getting so angry with me. I only thought you might like to hear what Michael was willing to pay for your house. I thought I was doing you a favor."

"But it only created trouble for us," said Louise firmly. "It was meddlesome."

"I'm sure Aunt Ethel didn't realize it would cause such a problem for us," suggested Alice.

Aunt Ethel's chin quivered as she offered up a grateful smile to Alice. "I really didn't mean to make trouble for you girls. Goodness, you three must know how much I love you."

"I'm sure that you do love us, Aunt Ethel," said Louise, softening a bit. "But sometimes it doesn't feel like it."

Aunt Ethel looked down at the floor.

"Another thing, Aunt Ethel," began Jane.

"Yes?" Aunt Ethel looked up.

"Well, we'd appreciate it if you didn't repeat so many things that happen within our family around the town."

"But I'm just a naturally friendly person," said Aunt Ethel. "You all know how much I love to chat with people. Goodness knows, even Lloyd calls me his social butterfly." Now she paused and carefully studied the three of them. "I suppose I didn't realize we have so many family secrets to hide." Her brows lifted in a slightly challenging expression.

"Oh, it's not that we have secrets," said Alice. "We just want you to respect our privacy a bit more. Is that too much to expect?"

"You know Acorn Hill, Alice. Everyone pretty much knows everything about everyone. That's just the way it is."

"Thanks to people who gossip," said Jane.

"*Harrumph*," Aunt Ethel snorted.

"I know it's not pleasant to hear these things, Aunt Ethel, and you need to understand that we all love you and are only saying this because we want to have a good relationship with you," Alice said. "Do you remember what Father used to say about gossip?"

Aunt Ethel nodded in what seemed a truly contrite manner. "My dear brother liked to remind everyone that gossip was as much a sin as murder or stealing."

Alice waited a few moments for this piece of truth to sink in before she added, "He also reminded us that Jesus forgives us when we admit we're wrong."

Aunt Ethel looked at Alice with what appeared to be honest-to-goodness tears now. "You are absolutely right, Alice, and I'm so sorry." Then she turned toward the other two. "I apologize to both of you, Louise and Jane. Honestly, I really don't want to see you girls sell your house and move away. I guess it's true that I did let my mouth run away with me again. Truly I didn't mean to hurt any of you." She wiped her nose with her tissue. "I guess I just like to feel involved."

"We want you to be involved, Aunt Ethel," said Alice. "You're family and we love you."

Louise and Jane both nodded.

"That's right," agreed Louise. "We do love you."

"Yes," said Jane. "And we need you too."

"Oh, you girls," said Aunt Ethel happily. "I don't ever want you to move away from here. Sometimes I feel closer to you three than my very own children."

Soon they were all hugging, and Alice felt that all was forgiven. Of course, she knew Aunt Ethel well enough to know that her tongue could easily get out of control again, but then they would just have to deal with that when it happened. Sometimes the best part of being part of a family was the ability to forgive and forget.

"Do you suppose you could straighten this little mess out with Mike Wall?" asked Louise as the four of them finally shared a pot of tea together.

Aunt Ethel nodded. "Certainly."

"And with Lloyd Tynan too?" asked Jane.

"I'll explain to both of them that you three have absolutely no intention of selling your house."

"Thank you," said Alice.

Then Aunt Ethel got a sparkle in her eye. "But what would you think if Mike Wall really offered you a million dollars for it?"

Alice glanced uncomfortably at her two sisters. Would a sum as large as a million dollars tempt either of them to sell out? Louise was already shaking her head in a firm "no."

"There are some things in life that money can't buy," said Jane with what sounded like heartfelt conviction.

Alice smiled in relief. "And our family is one of them."

Aunt Ethel smiled. "You three are most definitely your father's daughters."

Chapter Nineteen

*J*im Sharp started refinishing the hardwood floors during the week of Thanksgiving and didn't expect to be done for another week. No matter how hard the sisters tried to keep things clean, everything seemed coated with a fresh layer of sawdust by the following day. It was bad timing, but then the floors were in terrible condition and this job had to be done.

"I don't see why he couldn't have waited until next week," complained Jane as she wiped the coat of dust from the teakettle. "I'd really been looking forward to cooking a traditional Thanksgiving dinner this year. Usually we did something trendy and exotic at the restaurant. I've been hoping for good old-fashioned turkey and dressing, with homemade cranberry sauce and candied yams."

"Sounds good to me," said Louise.

"How about cooking a meal like that at the church?" suggested Alice. "I know that there are a number of people in town who are alone on Thanksgiving. As usual, the

ANGELs are preparing food baskets for the needy, but maybe we could do something even better this year."

"What a great idea, Alice," agreed Jane. "I love cooking for a crowd."

"Are you sure?" asked Louise. "It sounds like a lot of work."

"Oh, but it would be fun." Jane looked at Alice. "How many people do you suppose we could expect?"

"Oh, I'm not sure, but I could find out pretty easily. I doubt that it would be more than, say, twenty, maybe thirty at the most. Does that sound like too much?"

Jane shook her head. "Piece of cake."

"We can all help out, Jane," Alice reassured her. "And maybe my ANGELs would be interested in helping to serve that day."

"That would be great."

Louise looked as if she felt left out now. "Perhaps you'd like me to play some music for the event?"

"Oh, Louise, that would be wonderful," said Jane.

"And I happen to make a pretty good pumpkin pie," she added.

"Fantastic. I'll make some pecan and apple and . . ." Jane went over to the table and began making a list.

"Well, I'm off to work," announced Alice. "I'll start contacting our potential guests. I suppose I could even ask Carlene to put a notice in Wednesday's paper."

"Well, we don't want this thing to get too big," warned Louise.

"Oh, the more the merrier," said Jane with a wave of her hand.

"But who's going to pay for it?" asked the ever practical Louise.

"Goodness," said Alice. "I hadn't given that much thought."

"Doesn't the church have a fund for things like this?" asked Jane.

"Yes," said Alice. "We do. I'll call Pastor Ley during my morning break and ask about it. Naturally, he'll need to give his okay before we proceed, but I'm sure he'll love the idea."

Alice was exactly right about Pastor Ley's reaction.

"That's a f-fine idea, Alice," he told her over the phone. "I know of s-several elderly p-people who should be invited. They may be s-some of the s-same ones you have in m-mind, but I'll m-make a l-list just in case."

Alice even invited some of her co-workers to join them. She knew of several hospital employees who might be alone for the holiday. Then she called Carlene and asked her about putting a notice in the *Acorn Nutshell*.

"I'd be glad to," said Carlene. "Fact is, I wasn't sure what I was going to do on Thanksgiving myself. Until last week, I thought I was going home to my parents, but they've decided to fly out to Arizona to visit my brother this year. I might just end up at Grace Chapel too."

"Great," said Alice. "We'd love to have you join us."

The next couple of days whizzed by for Alice. Between her work at the hospital, helping out at home, and shopping for their upcoming dinner, she was practically asleep before her head hit the pillow each night. Some of her ANGELs were able to help serve on Thursday afternoon, and they all helped to decorate the assembly room on Wednesday night. They skittered around the room, artfully adorning the tables with bright gold tablecloths, little pumpkins, gourds, Indian corn and candles. Alice thought the room had never looked more festive. Just to be on the safe side, Alice had set the tables with forty-eight place settings. She figured they'd have some empty spots, but felt that was preferable to not having enough. She didn't want anyone to feel left out. Jane and Louise and even Aunt Ethel had been cooking for days. Not only that, but when others in the congregation heard about the dinner, they had offered to drop something by too.

"We'll probably have way too much food," said Jane. "Maybe we can send doggy bags home with our guests."

"Yes," agreed Louise as she pulled another pumpkin

pie from the oven. "The worst thing about eating Thanksgiving dinner at someone else's home is that you miss out on the leftovers."

Thanks to Jane's expertise and punctuality, everything was ready at two o'clock sharp. The first half hour was supposed to be for socializing and appetizers, and the real dinner was to begin at two-thirty. Louise, already seated at the piano, was thumbing through sheet music, while Alice coached her ANGELs on proper serving techniques. Before long a few guests began to trickle in. Alice greeted a couple of young co-workers from the hospital, as well as Cyril Overstreet. Taking their coats, she showed them to the appetizer table. She was beginning to feel a bit concerned. What if only a handful of people showed up today? Poor Jane, how would she feel if all her lovely food went to waste? Suddenly Alice remembered the story that Jesus had told about the rich man who gave a big fancy dinner, but nobody came. The desperate host had sent his servants out in the streets to invite more guests. She figured that the few streets of Acorn Hill would be fairly deserted right now.

Then more people began coming in. Carlene from the newspaper showed up with a basket of wheat rolls. And Hope from the Coffee Shop appeared with a hot blackberry pie. Alice graciously took their offerings, but at the same time fretted that she'd have to send them back home with them since there was already far more than enough food here. Then Viola from the bookstore showed up with a young family that had recently moved to town. Alice had heard that the father had suffered a back injury and the mother was looking for work.

Soon the basement was bustling with people and noise. Even Fred and Vera decided to come, explaining to Alice that both their girls had been invited home by college chums. "We were feeling a little lonely," confessed Vera as she handed Alice a casserole dish of yams. "Let me know if I can lend a hand with anything."

"Oh, I'm so glad you came," said Alice.

Alice took the hot dish to the kitchen and asked Jane if she needed any help.

"The place looks packed," said Jane as she pulled an extra pan of turkey dressing from the oven. "Have you done a nose count yet?"

Alice nodded. "Yes, and I think it was nearly sixty now. Can you believe it? And I was worried that we'd have way too much food. I already asked Sarah and Ashley to set another table."

"Oh my, I hope we have enough food for that many people," said Aunt Ethel as she paused from mashing pota-toes and glanced out across the crowded room. "Good grief,

Alice, there's another whole bunch more coming down the stairs right now. You better do another count."

Alice went back out and continued to greet people, smiling and taking coats, and all the time counting. This time she made it to nearly eighty. Eighty people! She was stunned. How was it that so many people were alone or in need? She hurried back to the kitchen to inform the others.

"My word!" exclaimed Aunt Ethel. "Eighty people? I thought you were only expecting about thirty."

"We weren't really sure," said Alice.

"But how will we manage to feed everyone?" said Aunt Ethel.

Alice grinned. "Remember the loaves and the fishes, Auntie."

"You better inform Pastor Ley that he needs to say one mighty impressive blessing," said Aunt Ethel.

Alice went out to tell the ANGELs to set up another long table with twenty more place settings. They had long since run out of paper plates and plastic utensils, but fortunately the church's kitchen was equipped with about forty sets of real dishes and silverware. Of course, this meant that someone would have to wash up now. But that seemed to be of little consequence at the moment.

Next Alice located Pastor Ley and his wife. "Quite a crowd, isn't it?" she whispered.

"This is quite a gathering you've pulled together, Alice," said Patsy.

Alice nodded with wide eyes. "Believe me, I'm as surprised at the turnout as anyone."

"W-wouldn't your father have loved this?" said Pastor Ley as he adjusted his wire-rimmed glasses. "I don't know w-why we didn't do something like this long ago."

"We didn't have Jane then," said Alice. "She's the cook in the family."

"Speaking of cooks," whispered Patsy, "you sure you'll have enough food? I brought a ham, but I could run home and get something else if you think—"

"No, no, Patsy," said Alice. "You just stay put." She turned to Pastor Ley now. "I was just reminding Aunt Ethel of the loaves and fishes. I told her I'd ask you to say a special blessing."

He grinned. "I'd be h-happy to invite the Good Lord to help us out."

Alice had already asked Lloyd Tynan to use his public speaking ability to get the crowd's attention, perhaps tell a few jokes and invite everyone to take their seats before he gave them an official welcome.

"We thank you all for coming," said Lloyd in his authoritative voice after the guests had been seated. "It's a pleasure to see you all here today. We had no idea we'd have such a fine group." He glanced toward the kitchen. "Maybe this will become a Grace Chapel tradition, although we better not mention this to the cooks just yet as it seems they have their hands full." This brought a few laughs. "Now, I'd like to ask Pastor Ley to say grace."

Pastor Ley nodded and bowed his head. "Dear heavenly F-father, we gather here today to give You th-thanks. We have so m-much to be th-thankful for . . . for our family and f-friends and community . . . for all this f-fine food and the hands that prepared it today. And we ask You to b-bless it—in the same way You b-blessed those loaves and f-fishes so many centuries ago. We ask that we m-might all leave this p-place f-filled with good food and good f-fellowship. Amen."

A hearty "amen" echoed throughout the basement. It wasn't long before everyone had a full plate of turkey, dressing, potatoes and gravy. Meanwhile, the ANGEL servers skittered about the tables bringing additional baskets of rolls, salads and a variety of other side dishes.

Louise and Alice finally took seats near Aunt Ethel and Lloyd and the Humberts, but Jane insisted upon staying in the kitchen.

"It's just my way," she had assured them. "I can't relax and eat until all of my customers—I mean guests—have eaten their last bite of dessert."

"Everything is delicious," said Vera.

Fred nodded. "I guess if we couldn't have Polly and Jean at home, this is the next best thing."

"Church should be like an extended family," said Louise. "I never really experienced that with our large congregation back in Philadelphia, but I've always felt that way here at home."

"Acorn Hill is just that kind of town," said Lloyd. "It makes you feel right at home."

"It sure does," said Jim Sharp from the other end of the table. "I've only been here three months and I feel like I know half the people in town already."

"You probably do," said Lloyd. "It only takes a week or two."

Aunt Ethel laughed. "We always tell newcomers to hang out at the hardware store if you want to get acquainted with folks."

"Thanks," said Fred. "I appreciate the business."

"It's true," said Lloyd. "Sooner or later, everyone in Acorn Hill goes into the hardware store."

"You got that right," said Jim. "I should know since I've been in there almost every single day these past two months."

"How's the renovation coming along?" asked Lloyd as he helped himself to another roll. "I haven't been by for a while. You got that roof replaced yet?"

Jim shook his head. "Afraid we'll have to wait until spring now that the cold weather's set in."

"Bet that's going to be one expensive little job," said Lloyd, blowing a low whistle through his teeth.

Louise nodded. "Don't we know it, but we can't very well run a first-rate inn with the rain coming down through the roof, now can we?"

"Daniel was lucky it held up this long," said Aunt Ethel. "I think that roof's about as old as the house."

Jim nodded. "Yep. Some of the worst sections of slate have been replaced over the years, but most of it's in pretty bad shape."

"I've been wondering about the church's roof too," said Fred. "I expect it won't be long before it'll need replacing too. Now, that's going to be an expensive job."

Alice felt uncomfortable with all this talk of repairs and money. "How are your girls doing, Vera?" she asked. "Does Polly like college?"

"She was pretty homesick, you know, but then she made a good friend. That's who she went home with for the weekend. The girl's family lives in Connecticut. And, of course, Jean went home to meet her boyfriend's family. We're not too sure what to make of that just yet." She gently elbowed her husband.

Fred made a groaning noise and shook his head. "I told

those girls I didn't want them to even think about getting married before they graduated from college and found themselves a decent-paying job."

Alice laughed. "Doesn't always work out that way, Fred."

"That's right," Vera reminded him. "Remember we got married during my second year of college."

"At least you finished up your degree," said Fred. "And you started teaching just as soon as you graduated."

"So will Polly and Jean," she assured him.

Alice checked from time to time to see how the food was holding out. There was still plenty for everyone. And they hadn't even brought out the desserts yet! Jane was in her element, and the compliments were flowing fast.

When it was all said and done, and everyone was as well stuffed as the turkeys had been, there were still leftovers. Alice felt certain that there must have been at least twelve baskets full! She asked Lloyd to announce that everyone was welcome to take leftovers home with them if they liked, and most of their guests happily obliged them.

Louise played piano while dessert and coffee were served, and most of the people sat around and visited for at least another hour. Then when it was time to clean up, several of the guests insisted that Jane should sit down while they commandeered the kitchen. Jane didn't protest and

Alice made sure that the ANGELs brought Jane everything she wanted as she sat with her sister.

"That was a beautiful meal," she told Jane as she sipped a cup of hot tea.

"Thanks, but it was only partly due to my efforts." Jane took a bite of yams. "For instance, I didn't make these, but they're really good." She glanced around the slowly thinning room. "A lot of people must've brought food with them today."

Alice smiled. "Good thing too."

Jane nodded. "*Great* thing!"

"I honestly believe God blessed our food too," said Alice. "Just like the loaves and fishes. We had a lot of people to feed."

"I have no doubt about that either." Jane forked a tender-looking piece of turkey and smiled.

"Really?"

"Yeah. I took a quick inventory before the dinner ever started. After all these years, I'm no fool when it comes to calculating amounts of food against the appetites of my customers, Alice. I have to admit I was honestly worried that we'd run out of turkey before all of our guests had even been served once."

"But there was plenty—enough for seconds."

Jane nodded with wide eyes. "I know. It was truly amazing."

"A miracle, do you think?"

"Oh, I don't know."

Alice sighed. "Well, I like to imagine Father up there in heaven, Jane. I envision him looking down on us and seeing we're in trouble. Then he turns around and says to God, 'Could You give them a hand down there?'"

Jane laughed. "You think?"

Chapter Twenty

*E*very day felt like Christmas to Alice once the hardwood floors were finally refinished, and since it was
December this seemed entirely appropriate. It got so that
she expected a new surprise each evening when she came
home from work. It had started with the dining room during the first week of December. Jane finished painting the
walls, then she and Louise spent the rest of the day putting
the room back together. The results were amazing.

Alice actually gasped when she saw the rich dark
mahogany wainscoting and trim contrasted against the
upper walls, freshly painted a soothing tone of pale green.
The golden wood floor seemed to glow with life and the
old Queen Anne style dining room furniture looked better
than new with its chair seats recovered in a subtle pale
green and ivory damask.

"Did you do the chair seats?" Alice asked Jane.

"Louise helped me," said Jane with a wide grin.

"I now know how to wield a staple gun," said Louise
proudly.

"Wow." Alice looked at the ivory lace panels that hung from the windows. "Lace?" She eyed Jane curiously. "You actually allowed lace?"

Jane nodded. "A few well-chosen pieces of lace can be quite charming."

"I talked her into it," said Louise with a childlike excitement. "These were panels from my old house in Philadelphia. Handmade in Scotland."

"I wasn't too excited about the idea at first," admitted Jane. "Then Louise pulled out those absolutely gorgeous pieces of lace. How could I refuse?"

"They fit perfectly." Louise smiled.

"And your rug, Louise," said Alice as she admired the ivory-colored rug with its delicate floral border. "It's absolutely wonderful in here."

"Isn't it grand?"

"You've even done a flower arrangement," said Alice as she went to examine the delicate flowers and crystal vase. "Just like in the book."

"Actually, Craig Tracy from Wild Things helped me with that," said Jane.

Alice bent to smell the lilies.

"He really knows his flowers," said Jane. "He even promised to help me with a cutting garden out back. He's got all kinds of seeds, and he said if I'm a good enough gardener, he might even buy blooms from me for his shop. I'm already starting a few seedlings in the sunroom."

"So." Louise folded her arms across her front. "What do you think of our first finished room, Alice?"

"I think it's absolutely beautiful, of course." Alice shook her head. "Far better than I'd ever imagined."

"Don't you think Mother would've loved this?" Louise's eyes were bright.

"Most definitely. It even goes with her fine china."

"I just put those on the sideboard for fun," said Jane. "I don't plan to actually use them for the inn. We'll need something more practical and dishwasher safe."

"But pretty," added Louise.

Jane nodded. "Yes. Maybe something in a celadon green. That would go well with the walls and it usually looks nice with most kinds of food."

"I think the cook should get to pick the dishes," said Alice.

"With approval," added Louise.

"I'm not sure about this table," said Jane. "I know we can add the leaves and seat up to twelve people but I was wondering about fitting several smaller tables in here instead. So people could dine in groups. But we'd still use these chairs."

"Do you think we could fit several tables in here?" asked Alice.

Jane studied the room. "I'm not sure."

"I like the idea of everyone eating at the same table," said Louise. "Sort of like inns in the old days. You get to know people that way. Remember how much fun everyone had at our Thanksgiving dinner, seated at those long tables? I can just imagine everyone sitting around here and chatting over one of Jane's fabulous breakfasts."

"You're right," said Alice.

"Well, maybe that's what we'll do for starters," agreed Jane. "It might be fun."

Then Jane started working on her kitchen. One day Alice came home to discover new black and white checkerboard tiles on the floor. They were bright and lively and fun.

"This is cheerful," she told Jane.

"Louise isn't too sure about it," said Jane. "I told her not to judge it until I'm all done in here."

"Well, it's your kitchen," said Alice. "I think it's important that you feel comfortable in here."

By the end of the week, Jane had painted the old wooden cabinets a bright paprika color and had glued several rows of colorful tiles along the backsplash. "It gives it a more contemporary feel, don't you think, Alice?"

Alice smiled. "Yes, but it's sort of old-fashioned too. Those tiles remind me of an Amish quilt."

"Exactly." Jane pointed to the wrought iron pot rack, loaded with all sorts of pots. "What do you think of this?"

"I like it." Alice ran her hand over the old maple countertops. "I'm glad you left the original butcher block."

Jane nodded. "That's one of the best features of this kitchen—that and the big soapstone sink. I would never change those things." She pointed to the old cookstove. "That, however, has got to go. I've already ordered a beauty. It should be here before Christmas. Stainless steel with eight burners. Amazingly, it's exactly the right size for the space."

"Well, that old stove's huge." Alice glanced at their refrigerator. It hadn't been replaced since the fifties. "What about that dinosaur?"

Jane laughed. "It's history. I've got a Sub-Zero coming too, as well as an industrial-strength dishwasher. You can't even get a permit to run a restaurant without one of those things."

"Expensive?" asked Alice.

Jane nodded. "We can be thankful that Louise, or rather Eliot, was such a good investor."

"Are you talking about me again?" Louise came in to join them.

"I was just showing Alice my latest improvements," said Jane.

"What do you think of it, Louise?" asked Alice.

"Well, I must admit that the cabinet color feels warm and cozy." Louise glanced around the kitchen. "And those tiles are growing on me. The new floor looks much better with everything else in place."

"Did you see my curtains?" asked Jane as she pointed out the neat linen panels trimmed with stripes of red, blue and green that matched the colors of the wall tiles.

"Those are cute," said Alice. "Where did you get them?"

"I made them from some dish towels I found in a catalog."

"Dish towels?" Louise stepped closer to see. "My word, she did. Why, Jane, you are such a clever girl."

"Well, I just totally love it in here now," said Jane. "It makes me really feel like cooking."

"It makes me feel like smiling," said Alice.

Unfortunately the second floor, with the four guest bedrooms, was still quite a mess. Some progress had been made with wallpaper stripping and some of the trim painting had been done, but the hardwood floors still needed refinishing and the plumbing fixtures were in various phases of removal and replacement. Alice tried not to look too hard as she walked past this floor and on up to her bedroom above. It was hard seeing things so torn up. It was some comfort having their private bedrooms now intact. At least she and her sisters always had a place to go when all the other rooms in the house were in a state of chaos, cluttered with ladders and tools and layers of sawdust.

"Now if only the roof can hold out until spring," said Alice as the three of them sat down to dinner in the festive kitchen.

"I wish Jim could get to it sooner," said Louise. "What if we have bad snow or freezing this year?"

"Can you imagine what a mess that will make of all our other improvements?" said Jane.

"Well, it would hit the attic first," said Alice. "I suppose we could put lots of buckets and barrels up there if it does. I had to do that in a couple of spots last winter, although it wasn't too bad. Come to think of it, I'm sure the buckets are still up there right now."

"Goodness," said Louise. "I hope we can hold out."

"Let's hope that spring comes early," said Alice.

"Aunt Ethel stopped by to check on our improvements today," said Jane.

"What did she think of your kitchen?" asked Louise, fork poised in midair.

"She thought I'd made some big mistake. *'Land sake, this can't possibly be a color you'd have chosen, Jane,'* she said to me in perfect Aunt Ethel horror." Jane laughed. "I told her that I picked it out myself, and she said, 'Why, I thought you were an artist, dear.' *Sheesh!*" Jane rolled her eyes. "She really knows how to make a girl feel good."

"I thought Aunt Ethel liked vibrant colors," said Alice. "You've seen how she dresses."

Louise shrugged. "Apparently she likes to wear them, but not to decorate with them."

"Speaking of décor," said Jane, "some of the wallpapers came today. Louise and I already took a peek, but you might like to see them, Alice."

Soon dinner was done, and Jane got out the boxes of paper and pulled out several rolls. "Here's the stripe for the foyer," she announced as she unrolled a strip of pale gold and ivory stripes and laid it across the dining room table. "Doesn't this have a lovely sheen to it?"

Alice ran her hand over the smooth paper. "It's beautiful."

Louise didn't look completely satisfied. "I still think I would've preferred something with more life to it."

"Just wait until you see it up," said Jane. "It'll be perfect."

"Are you really going to hang it yourself?" asked Alice.

"I've done it before," said Jane. "But I think I'll start with one of the smaller projects first, like the parlor. Besides, I may need Jim to help me with the high walls in the foyer."

"Oh, you must see the parlor paper," said Louise suddenly. "It's my favorite one by far." She reached into a box and dramatically unfurled a roll of paper.

Alice studied the delicate rows of green ivy and pale lavender violets. "It's pretty," she said.

"I know it's not Jane's first choice," said Louise. "But I

think it goes nicely with the parlor. It has a lovely border that will go around the ceiling."

Jane shrugged. "It might look better than I expect. If not, you won't find me hanging out in the parlor much." She laughed. "Not that I do anyway."

"That brings me to another concern," said Louise. "I've been thinking that it might be better to use the parlor for my music lessons. I was looking at the rooms the other day, and I thought it might be nice to keep Father's study as a library. It would be a nice quiet place for guests to go and read or write or borrow a good book."

"I'm not sure how quiet it will be with kids hammering on the piano right next door," said Jane.

Louise's brows lifted. "Hammering?"

Jane grinned. "You know what I mean."

"My pupils do not hammer," said Louise sternly. Then she smiled. "I only plan to teach those with the true ability to play. My poor old ears are too finely tuned to suffer through anything less than that."

"Well, that's a relief," said Jane.

"Speaking of piano music," said Louise. "I told Aunt Ethel and Lloyd that we might have a little sing-along music on Christmas Eve—if the house is somewhat ready by then. What do you think, Jane?"

"I think a sing-along would be great."

"I mean about the house." Louise peered into the dimly lit and barren living room and frowned. "Is there really any chance that the downstairs will be presentable by Christmas?"

"I'm certain that the living room will be finished. There's even a chance that the parlor will be done, but I honestly don't see how I can get the wallpaper up in the foyer by then. The new stair runner isn't supposed to be here until after the New Year."

"I guess we can't have everything," said Alice.

Louise frowned. "I'm just getting so tired of living like vagrants."

Jane laughed. "I wouldn't exactly call us vagrants, Louise."

"Well, all this grimy dust and building debris." Louise shook her head. "It wears on my nerves."

"These things take time," said Jane with a frown. "And lately it's been just Jim and me working here, for the most part anyway."

"I'll be here for the rest of the week," said Alice. "I'm ready to be put to work again."

"I've been trying to help out in the house," said Louise, "but it seems I spend most of my time driving around and being your gofer these days."

"I know." Jane patted Louise on the back. "Sorry if I seem cranky. I guess I wish it were all done too. In the fall

I imagined all of us sitting around our beautifully reno-vated home by Christmastime. I thought I'd be baking all these lovely cookies and treats, but my new stove hasn't even arrived yet. Besides I don't have enough time to do much in the way of baking."

"Let's not push ourselves too hard," said Alice. "I think if we simply get the living room finished and put back together for the holidays, we'll be doing just fine. I plan to do everything I can during the next few days to help out."

"As do I," said Louise. "By the way, Cynthia called today, and she'd like to come visit for Christmas. I told her that the guest floor was still somewhat uninhabitable, but that she was welcome to share my room."

"Actually," said Jane with a twinkle in her eye, "the Sunset Room may be ready by then."

"Really?" Louise looked hopeful. "When could you have possibly had time to work on that?"

Jane smiled. "I wasn't going to mention it, but there are those nights when I can't get to sleep, so I sneak down there and putter around. I'm surprised I haven't disturbed you."

Alice chuckled. "I thought I heard something one night, and I meant to put out some mousetraps the next morning."

"You'd need quite large ones," said Jane.

"So when do we get to see your new creation?" asked Louise.

"Not until every single thing is in place."

"It is just like Christmas!" exclaimed Alice.

"What do you mean?" asked Louise.

"All these new rooms and renovations. Isn't it fun? Each time something gets done feels just like opening up a new package." Alice glanced around the finished dining room. "Like this room. I just love it so much. And your kitchen too, Jane. Honestly, if the other rooms only turn out half this nice I'll be completely happy."

Chapter Twenty-One

*G*race Chapel Inn seemed to turn a corner just before Christmas. To start with, as promised, Alice donned her coveralls and rolled up her sleeves and helped Jane attack the living room.

"I gave Louise enough errands to keep her out of the house for most of the day," confessed Jane as she masked off the wood trim. "I don't want her to see this room until the painting is completely done."

"What exactly do you have in mind?" asked Alice as she studied the cans of various colors of paint on the drop cloth.

"Remember when you asked me about faux painting? Well, we're going to do a faux finish in here." Jane was already opening the cans. "And we need to work quickly, Alice."

"Aye-aye, sir," said Alice with a mock salute.

Jane stood up and smiled. "That's just the attitude I'm looking for today. I need someone who can take orders and not ask a bunch of questions."

"At your service."

As she was instructed, Alice started rolling a pale

golden color onto the upper walls. Jane had already decided that the wainscoting, which had always been painted in that room, should simply remain painted, and she had covered it with a nice creamy white a few weeks ago. "Don't worry about getting that gold on evenly," she said. "Just smear it around diagonally. I'll follow you with the next step."

So Alice did her best to smear the paint around, but she couldn't help being concerned that it didn't look very nice. Still, she kept her mouth shut and did as Jane instructed. She was so focused that she barely noticed Jane following behind her with a scrunched up rag and pan of paint. Finally, Alice completed the longest wall and turned to see how it looked.

"Oh my!" Alice looked at Jane's half of the wall and shook her head. "That is amazing, Jane. It looks beautiful, almost like marble or some sort of stone."

Jane paused to grin and push a stray strand of dark hair from her eyes. "Thanks. Now, back to work."

By one o'clock, they had finished the faux painting, and the living room glowed with color and warmth and elegance. "Oh, Jane!" Alice exclaimed. "I never dreamed it would be so pretty. How did you know?"

Jane winked and paused to add a finishing stroke with her wadded up cloth. "I'm the artist, remember?"

"No arguing with you there."

"So, how about if you start cleaning up, and I'll go see if Jim can help me move a few pieces of furniture in here. Wouldn't it be fun to have some things in place before Louise gets back? She was totally unconvinced that I was going to pull off this room."

Alice was already peeling masking tape and paper from the wainscoting. "She'll be convinced now." She paused to look at it once more. "You know what else, Jane? It looks really lovely with the dining room color right next door. The gold and the green seem complimentary. Did you plan that too?"

"Of course." Jane dropped her messy cloth into the garbage can. "I tried to pick out all the downstairs colors to go with each other. I hate it when you walk from one room to the next and it feels like you've entered an entirely different house."

Alice nodded. "Yes, that makes sense." Of course, Alice knew she never would have thought of such a thing herself, but she was glad that Jane had that vision.

It took Alice nearly an hour to clean and clear the living room of the paint debris. By then, Jane and Jim were carrying in some large pieces of furniture from the basement and attic.

"How about if I fix us a little lunch," suggested Alice as she watched Jane deciding on where to place the marble-topped table. "Since it's obvious that I'll be of little use in here."

"Sounds good," said Jane. "You in, Jim?"

"Never turn down free food," he said as he carefully edged the table next to the bay window. "Is that where you want it, Jane?"

"Perfect."

So Alice went into Jane's cheerful kitchen and poked around the refrigerator until she found some leftover mushroom soup and some sandwich meat. She knew her lunch didn't look as festive as something Jane would put together, but Jane and Jim seemed thankful just the same.

"What are your plans for Christmas?" Alice asked Jim.

"I thought I'd go visit my son," said Jim as he scraped his spoon across his bowl.

"I didn't know you have a son," said Alice.

"He has a daughter too," said Jane. "They live in Washington State."

Jim grinned. "Sounds like you've been paying attention to all my chitchat, Jane."

"I also remember that you have several grandchildren. The daughter has a new baby, and the son has two or three kids."

"Two." Jim nodded. "Two girls."

"Well, that's nice," said Alice. "You're a grandpa."

"Yep. My son and his wife have been begging me to

come see them in their new home. And I haven't even seen my daughter's baby yet."

"Now, I know about your kids, Jim," began Jane. "But you've never mentioned a wife. What's the story there?"

He frowned. "Divorce."

Jane nodded as she picked up the empty plates. "I know how that goes. You don't have to talk about it if you don't want to."

"Thanks."

"Well, you two can feel free to get back to whatever you were doing," said Alice. "I'll clean up in here."

"Great." Jane set down the plates in the sink. "Louise might be home any minute now."

Alice puttered around in the kitchen. She really liked how warm and cheerful it felt in there now. It was so much nicer than before. She wondered why it had never occurred to her to paint the cabinets such a nice bright color. *That's just me*, she thought as she rinsed out a soup bowl.

"Hello?" called Louise from the front foyer.

Alice dried off her hands and hurried out to see her older sister's reaction. You could never be certain with Louise.

"Oh my!" Louise's hand flew to her mouth as she walked into the living room. She stood in the center and turned around and just looked with wide eyes. Alice couldn't tell if she was pleased or horrified. "Oh my!" she said again.

Alice looked around the room and smiled. She thought it looked perfectly lovely. The sofa and overstuffed chair reupholstered in burgundy fabric looked elegant with several new pillows in place, as well as a beautiful knitted throw in shades of burgundy, cream and gold. Their mother's antique rocker looked at home in the corner, and Jane had even taken time to place a potted fern on the marble-topped table by the window. Well, Alice thought the room looked absolutely sensational.

"It's perfect," breathed Louise as she finally peeled off her gloves.

"Really?" Jane went over and threw her arms around Louise. "You honestly think so? I have a few more pieces to put into place and some things for the wall and—"

Louise nodded and just mutely turned around again. "*Honestly.* It is heavenly, Jane. How did you know how to do this?"

"Remember, she's an artist," said Alice, winking at Jane.

"I haven't got it all together yet," said Jane, "but I think you can get the effect I'm going for."

"We get it, Jane," Alice assured her.

"Alice was right," said Louise happily. "It is like Christmas. Now, if someone will help me to unload the car."

"Let me," offered Alice. "I think Jane is more useful in here."

As it turned out, even Aunt Ethel loved the living room. When Jane took the time to add a few Christmas touches, like the trio of alabaster angels that had belonged to their mother, lots of creamy white candles in brass candlestick holders, and with plenty of evergreen boughs, holly and pine cones along the big oak mantle, the room looked festive and ready for the holidays.

Then the following week, Alice came home to discover that Father's study, now called "The Daniel Howard Library," was wallpapered with a friendly tweed in mossy shades of green and brown.

"That wallpaper looks so nice next to the mahogany woodwork," said Alice when her two sisters showed her the room. "It makes the rich color of the wood literally gleam in contrast."

"That's thanks to Louise," said Jane. "She spent the last two days cleaning and oiling the bookshelves. She's even been rearranging the books."

"Just putting them in a more orderly fashion," explained Louise. "So we can find titles more easily."

"Where did this area rug come from?" asked Alice as she admired the Oriental rug in shades of rust and gold and black.

"Don't you remember?" asked Louise. "It used to be in Mother and Father's bedroom."

"Oh yes. It always seemed a bit dark for a bedroom, but I like it in here." Alice pointed to the pair of russet colored chairs across from the desk. "And those are from the bedroom too?"

"Yes," admitted Jane. "They were like new. I don't think Father ever sat on them once. Don't they go well in here?"

Alice nodded. "You are a whiz, Jane."

"Louise sewed the cushion covers," said Jane.

Alice picked up one of the decorative pillows. It was a geometric design tapestry of earthy greens and gold. "What beautiful fabric."

"Jane found that at Sylvia's Buttons," said Louise. "At first I thought it looked too contemporary, but I like it now."

Alice looked around the room in satisfaction, her eyes settling on the big mahogany desk where her father's old black leather Bible and dated globe still sat. "I think Father would like it in here."

"Really?" Jane looked hopeful. "I tried to keep him in mind. I didn't want to do anything with this room that felt unlike him."

"You did a great job." Alice sighed, feeling slightly left out. "I just wish I could've been more help."

"You've been wonderful help," said Jane. "Your encouragement and diplomatic skills. Really, we never would've gotten this far without you."

Alice forced a smile to her lips. Maybe it wasn't just a feeling of being left out. Maybe it was simply the fresh reminder that Father was gone. His study was no longer the same. He was not coming back, but then what did she expect? She absently gazed at the blank wall directly behind his desk and then pointed to it. "What do you plan to do with that, Jane?"

Jane frowned. "I'm not sure. I agree with you that it needs something."

"I have an idea," said Alice suddenly.

"Really?" Louise looked skeptical.

"Yes. I saw something like it at the hospital once. Old Henry Tyler had suffered a pretty bad heart attack and his daughter, I think her name is Lucy, brought in this large framed picture. It was a sepia-toned photo of old Henry as a boy, going fishing. It was about this big." Alice held her hands about two feet apart. "I asked Lucy about it, and she said it was an old snapshot that she'd gotten blown up at a professional photocopy shop. They had some really nice machine, not like our copier at the hospital, but the good kind that they use for photography. Anyway, I have some old snapshots of Father when he was a boy, and also during his days at seminary, as well as a few from when he and Mother first met. Suppose we picked some of those and had them blown up and nicely framed and—"

"Alice!" exclaimed Jane. "You are a genius! That is an absolutely brilliant idea."

Alice beamed.

"I know just the place to have it done," said Louise. "There's a shop in Philadelphia that a friend of mine runs. I'll have them sent out and back in no time."

"See," said Alice. "It's still just like Christmas."

In the next two weeks, the parlor was completed, with the ivy and violet wallpaper hung to Louise's satisfaction, and all the furnishings in place, including Louise's baby grand piano. Not only that, but the cookies also got baked. They were not as spectacular as Jane would have liked but were temptingly tasty just the same. Then, with less than a week before Christmas, a tall fir tree was put up in the parlor, complete with twinkling lights and some handblown antique ornaments. By Christmas Eve, the three sisters were finally ready for their sing-along—*and* a long winter's nap.

Chapter Twenty-Two

*C*ynthia is here!" Louise sang out as she rushed through the foyer to answer the doorbell. "Come and say hello to my one and only daughter."

Alice set down a heaping platter of Christmas cookies on the dining room table and then hurried out to greet her niece. "Welcome home!" she said as she hugged Cynthia and helped her with her coat. "Did you have a good trip?"

"The traffic was awful until I got to Acorn Hill." Cynthia looked around the foyer and frowned. "Hey, I thought you guys were fixing this place up."

Louise laughed. "Don't judge a house by its foyer. We're still a work in progress. Come and see the living room and dining room and say hello to Jane. Then we'll give you the full tour."

"Oh my," said Cynthia as they walked into the candlelit living room. "This is *really* beautiful." She walked around the room in wonder.

"It's mostly Jane's doing," said Louise. "Although we all

helped out a little. I even sanded the woodwork a bit myself before Jane painted it."

"It feels almost celestial in here," Cynthia finally said after she had examined everything. "What a totally amazing transformation. I can hardly believe this is the same house."

"We considered putting the Christmas tree in here," said Louise, "but decided to stay with family tradition and have it in the parlor."

"I like it this way," admitted Alice. "With all the candles and the greenery on top of the mantle, I think this room is lovely without a tree."

"Now come see the dining room," said Louise, her eyes sparkling like a little girl. "It's lovely too."

"Wow," said Cynthia as they went into the dining room. "Everything looks so different from the last time I was here." She shook her head in amazement. "Everything feels so much lighter and brighter—I absolutely love it! I may never want to go home."

"Hello," called Jane as she pushed open the swinging doors from the kitchen. "How are you, Cynthia?"

"Worn out," she said as she hugged Jane. "You look really good, Aunt Jane. I love that dress."

Jane set down a tray of cheese and crackers and then held out the full skirt of her burgundy velveteen dress. "I got this in a retro shop in San Francisco a few years ago. Almost forgot I had it."

"Goodness, Jane, does that mean it's actually been *used*?" asked Louise in a horrified voice.

Jane grinned. "Yep. That's what makes it so special."

"There are a couple shops like that in Boston," said Cynthia. "I couldn't work up the nerve to go, but maybe I will now."

"You would wear *used* clothing?" Louise looked aghast.

Cynthia laughed. "Come on, Mom, get with the program."

"Speaking of program, we better continue our tour," Alice said, "before our other guests begin arriving."

"Yes," agreed Louise, "but Cynthia should take a peek at Aunt Jane's kitchen first."

"It's a little messy at the moment," said Jane as she led them into it. "I've been a baking maniac today."

"Oh, Aunt Jane, it's adorable. I love these bright colors, and this floor is very cool. What fun! It actually makes me want to cook."

"Now, that'd be something," said Louise. "Considering you barely know how to make toast."

"Maybe Jane should give Cynthia some lessons while she's here," suggested Alice.

"I'm afraid Aunt Jane would pull her hair out," confessed Cynthia. "I'm really pretty hopeless in the kitchen. Although I do peel a mean potato."

"All right," said Louise. "Let's keep this tour moving. You have to see the library and parlor now, Cynthia."

Cynthia paused to read the sign on the door to the library. "The Daniel Howard Library." She pushed open the heavy paneled door and went in. "This is really nice. It makes me want to curl up and read a good book."

"That's just the look we were going for."

Next they went to the parlor. "This is my favorite room," said Louise proudly. "Don't you love this wallpaper?"

Cynthia nodded. "Yes, it feels like your style, Mom. Your beautiful piano looks completely at home in here." She paused by the Christmas tree. "What a lovely tree. Hey, I recognize that little angel playing the flute."

Louise laughed. "Yes, we've all contributed from our own collections."

Alice glanced around the parlor. The wallpaper really did look perfect in this room. Quaint and old-fashioned, but still light and cheerful. Much better than the old dark print that used to adorn the walls. "Now, let's help Cynthia get her bags up to the Sunset Room."

"Sunset Room?" Cynthia looked puzzled.

"Yes, dear, we named the guest rooms." Louise picked up the smaller overnight bag, and Alice got the larger one.

"Better hurry up, Jane," called Alice from the foyer. "We're heading up to see your special room now."

"Not without me," yelled Jane as she hurried toward the staircase. "Remember what I said."

Alice turned to Cynthia. "Jane has been so secretive. She wouldn't even let Louise or me see this room yet."

"That's because I only finished it this afternoon."

"It's the first guest room that's ready for visitors," said Louise.

"Right this way, girls." Jane led them up the stairs and down the hallway, before she opened the door with much aplomb. "Welcome to the Sunset Room."

"Oh, Jane," gushed Cynthia. "This is fabulous."

Alice looked around the spacious bedroom in wonder. What used to be an old set of worn bedroom furniture now had a creamy antiqued finish and looked elegant and comfortable. The walls were faux painted in terra cotta tones, giving it a warm, cozy feel. Some nicely matted and framed prints adorned the walls as if they had hung there forever. "How do you do this, Jane?" gushed Alice. "Honestly, it looks like a page out of *Beautiful Home* magazine."

"Don't you *love* this fabric?" said Jane as she happily plumped a blue, gold and terra cotta tapestry pillow. "Sylvia special-ordered it for me. It's kind of old-fashioned, but the colors feel contemporary."

"The whole room has such a warm and welcoming feel, Aunt Jane," said Cynthia. "I really feel honored to be the first person to use it."

"Well, don't feel too honored," said Jane. "Unfortunately the bathrooms on this floor aren't operable yet. You'll need to trek either upstairs or down to use the facilities, but you look like you're in pretty good shape to me."

"I don't mind a bit," said Cynthia. "Just using this pretty room makes me feel special. I can handle the stairs just fine."

"Goodness," said Louise with a worried frown. "I don't know if my guest room will be able to hold its own against this one."

"Maybe we should ask Jane to help us with our rooms," said Alice.

Louise nodded. "Perhaps you're right. She just seems to be getting better and better at this decorating business."

Jane laughed. "It's so much fun. Honestly, it's almost as rewarding as cooking. Although I have a feeling that once we're done, I may be tired of it. But you never know. I might have to take up decorating as a part-time job if the inn doesn't bring in enough business."

"I think I hear someone at the door," said Alice. "You three take your time up here and I'll let them in."

Since it was still a bit early, Alice suspected it was Aunt Ethel. Naturally, she was right. "Come right in, Auntie," she said with a big smile. "Merry Christmas!"

"Thank you, dear." Aunt Ethel peered over Alice's shoulder. "Is that Cynthia's car I see parked out front?"

Alice nodded. "They're upstairs admiring Jane's guest room."

"Oh, I must see it! That Jane," Aunt Ethel handed Alice her coat. "She's really got an artist's eye."

Alice chuckled to herself as she hung up her aunt's coat. It wasn't long ago that Aunt Ethel had insulted Jane over her choice of colors in the kitchen. *Just like the weather*, thought Alice as she went to put on another Christmas CD and check on the refreshment table.

Soon, Fred and Vera arrived with both their daughters in tow. Next came Hope, then Lloyd Tynan along with Pastor Ley and his wife Patsy. Alice had also invited members of the church board to come tonight, hoping that it might help allay some of their fears about their soon-to-be inn, but she really didn't expect that Florence Simpson and her husband Ronald would show up. She hoped her face didn't register too much surprise when she opened the door to see them on the porch.

"Florence," she said with a nervous smile. "And Ronald. Welcome to our home. Come in, come in."

Florence looked skeptically around the drab looking foyer. "I thought you were doing a renovation here." She handed Alice her heavy fur coat. Alice tried not to wince as she slipped the coat onto a sturdy hanger. She had never liked the feeling of animal fur, and tried to dispel the image of all the critters that had given up their luxurious pelts.

"The foyer won't be finished until after Christmas," she explained as she took Ronald's wool coat.

"Well, Alice," said Ronald. "Contrary to popular opinion, I happen to like what you've done with the exterior of your house."

"You do?" Alice glanced at Florence just in time to see her scowl.

He nodded. "I never thought that great big peach house looked appropriate next to the church. It almost seemed to upstage it, in my opinion."

Florence sniffed. "Well, it seemed like a part of Acorn Hill's history to me."

Alice thought it was time to change the subject. "Why don't you come and see the living room," she said quickly. "Jane is our decorator, and we all think she's done a pretty nice job."

She led them into the golden living area where a number of guests were mingling and admiring the renovations. "There are lots of goodies in the dining room," Alice assured the Simpsons. "Feel free to look around and see what we've done. We're still in progress, but I'm sure you'll see that we've—"

"I simply adore what Jane's done in the kitchen," said Hope as she grabbed Alice's arm. "I wish she could give the Coffee Shop a makeover like this."

Relieved at the interruption, Alice asked Hope if she had seen the library yet and then happily took her and several others to tour the other part of the downstairs as more guests arrived and were greeted by Jane and Louise.

Soon it was time for the sing-along, and Louise began directing everyone toward the parlor. "Time for caroling," she called merrily.

Alice had retreated to the kitchen for a brief respite from conversations. She was never at her best at parties and large social gatherings. Besides that, she knew that Jane would appreciate a bit of help cleaning up after her whirlwind day of cooking and baking for the party. She was just wiping down a counter when she overheard quiet voices in the dining room.

"Can you imagine that Pastor Daniel was able to tuck away this much money?" It was Florence Simpson talking in a hushed conspiring tone.

"It seems highly unlikely," said another voice that Alice immediately recognized as Clara Horn's—one of Grace

Chapel's most notorious gossips. Apparently Aunt Ethel had invited her friend Clara here tonight, a nice gesture since Clara was a recent widow and had no close family nearby. Alice was about to step through the swinging doors and make her presence known to the two women, but then paused for a moment. She knew she was eavesdropping, but somehow she just couldn't help herself.

"Well, it's obvious that his daughters are pouring a lot of hard-earned money into this showy remodeling project," said Florence. "I'm sure that Alice couldn't have saved up very much on her nurse's wages, and Jane just worked in a restaurant and couldn't have much cash set aside."

"I believe Louise and her husband made their living giving piano lessons," added Clara. "There's not much money in that. Yes, it does seem a bit strange that the Howard household should suddenly find themselves so well-heeled."

"I just read about a TV evangelist who embezzled millions from his ministry," said Florence. "Do you suppose that Pastor Daniel could've done something like that? You know how the church has always struggled to make ends meet. Could he have possibly been siphoning money off?"

Alice couldn't remember many times in her life when she had actually felt enraged enough to physically harm someone, but she believed she was coming mighty close

246 Tales from Grace Chapel Inn

right now. She put her hand on the door, ready to shove it open and make a dramatic appearance, but then she stopped herself.

"Pastor Daniel always *seemed* like a good man to me," said Clara with a trace of doubt in her voice. "But then you just never know about folks. The Bible speaks of wolves in sheep's clothing. And it does seem that his daughters are throwing a lot of money around making this place into some kind of fancy showplace. Regardless of where it came from, money like this would be much better spent helping out poor missionaries or even the church itself. I've heard Fred Humbert saying that the church roof is in bad need of replacement."

"I think something smells fishy," said Florence. "I plan to get to the bottom of it. Might even have to call an emergency board meeting."

Now Alice knew that she was far too angry to actually confront these two women without losing her temper. She had long ago learned from her father about the danger of approaching someone while still infuriated. He always gave himself a "cool down time" when something flared up amongst the congregation that got his dander up.

"Be angry and sin not," he would quote to Alice from the Bible. "I don't want to give the devil a chance to make this situation any worse than it already is." He was always right. If he gave himself enough time, he usually came up with the answers, and the wait never hurt anything.

So Alice slipped up the back staircase to her bedroom. She knew she needed to cool off a bit, although she wouldn't be able to hide out for long. Once safely in her room, she got down on her knees and asked God to help her through this trial. She asked Him to help her to control her anger as well as her tongue. Then, worried that Jane's sharp eyes would soon notice that she was missing from the group, she went back down and joined the jovial crowd of carolers now gathered around the piano in the parlor.

Naturally, it bothered her to see Florence and Clara standing with Lloyd and Aunt Ethel as they sang along with the others. She felt they were hypocritical participating in this party after they'd said such horrid things about her family. She took a deep breath as she carefully averted her eyes from the two women and attempted to focus her attention on the music and the joyful words of the old familiar Christmas carols.

Louise and Jane both looked so happy tonight. Alice knew she wouldn't trouble them with this unfortunate bit of news yet. It was bad enough that her spirits had been dampened, no need to spoil their holiday too. As the group sang "God Bless Ye Merry Gentleman," she wondered how her father would handle these two mean-spirited women.

Of course, she knew that whatever Father had ever said or done to remedy such malicious problems, he had always done so with grace. If anything, grace had been Father's main motto for living. It had always seemed to permeate all areas of his life and, quite properly, it was even the name of his beloved little church, and now their soon-to-be inn. Grace Chapel.

Grace, grace, grace. Alice sighed. *Dear God, help me.*

Chapter Twenty-Three

Alice decided to wait until after Christmas to do something about Florence and Clara's misguided and misinformed little gossip session. She figured a couple of days would prove a good cooling off period for her. But she knew she couldn't ignore this problem for too long. She had seen too many other incidents where serious damage had been inflicted when thoughtless gossip had spread like wildfire. And Alice had no desire to confront those two busybodies herself. Despite two days to cool off, she wasn't sure that she could control her temper when it came to someone slandering her beloved father. So on the day after Christmas, Alice walked over to Aunt Ethel's little carriage house and knocked on the door.

"Good morning, Alice," said Aunt Ethel in a cheery voice. "You're just in time for tea."

"Thank you," said Alice. "That would be nice."

After they had sat at Aunt Ethel's kitchen table and visited for a bit, Alice broached the subject. "Aunt Ethel, I have a problem," she began.

Her aunt frowned and leaned forward with keen interest. "What is it, dear? Are those two sisters of yours fighting again?"

Alice shook her head. "No, it's nothing like that. In fact, we had the best evening playing Scrabble with Cynthia last night. Naturally, Louise won."

"That Louise. She always manages to come up with some obscure word with a Z that she plants right over the triple word score."

"Yes, that's about how it went."

Aunt Ethel refilled Alice's cup. "But, tell me, Alice, what is troubling you?"

"Well, I accidentally overheard a conversation on Christmas Eve."

Aunt Ethel's eyes grew bright. "Accidentally?"

Alice sighed. "I really wasn't trying to eavesdrop. I was simply cleaning up in the kitchen and I heard Florence Simpson and Clara Horn talking in the dining room. I was about to go in and say something, but their conversation had already gone too far for me to make a graceful interruption."

Aunt Ethel nodded, eager to hear more. "What were they talking about?"

"It seems that they've gotten the crazy idea that Father may have, well, embezzled money from the church."

Aunt Ethel's teacup clanged against the saucer. "What on earth?"

"I know. It sounds terrible saying it out loud. But apparently they're suspicious about the renovations we've been doing in the house. They assumed that none of us would have enough money to do these repairs and improvements, and that perhaps Father had squirreled away some church funds that we are currently squandering."

"*Good night alive!*" Aunt Ethel blew air through her nostrils. "Of all the idiotic things to say!"

Alice nodded. "I know. Even though it's totally ridiculous, I just hate the idea of them spreading a vicious rumor like that—"

"Well, certainly! It's absolute nonsense."

"But I wasn't quite sure what to do. I was worried that I might lose my temper with them and only make matters worse. Then I remembered that they're friends of yours and I hoped maybe you could talk some sense into them."

"Well, I most definitely will."

"Without upsetting them?"

"*Humph.* I think they need to be upset a bit. The nerve of those two! Spreading such complete poppycock about our dear Daniel!"

"I thought about how Father would handle something like this . . . and then I remembered how he would often bring in a third party to settle a dispute. That's why I thought of you."

Aunt Ethel smiled and patted her hand. "You did exactly the right thing. Now, don't worry, dear, I won't go getting them all riled up either. I'll simply set the record straight with them. Perhaps Lloyd would like to join me. We could invite the two of them to meet us at the Coffee Shop—a public place is always the best place for something as potentially volatile as this." Aunt Ethel stood and patted her hair. "If you'll excuse me, I should probably get right on this before it gets any further out of hand."

"Thanks, Aunt Ethel." Alice smiled with relief. "I thought you'd know what to do."

"Of course, dear, this is right up my alley."

Alice knew that was true. Aunt Ethel was an expert when it came to gossip and rumors. Even though she never intended to inflict hurt, it might prove a good reminder to her of how easily these things can get out of hand.

Aunt Ethel chuckled as she reached for her coat and purse. "You know me, Alice, I've always enjoyed a juicy piece of gossip as much as anyone, but only when it's the truth. I do not approve—and never have approved—of out and out falsehoods."

Alice wanted to ask her aunt how she was able to discern the difference, but decided not to go there today. "Good luck," she said as she went out the door. "And remember to season your words with grace."

Aunt Ethel waved. "Yes, of course, dear."

Alice said a quick prayer for Aunt Ethel as she headed back home. She had decided not to trouble her sisters with this little predicament during the holidays and felt no need to make them feel bad now. She hoped that Aunt Ethel would nip it in the bud before the day was even over.

"Hey," called Jane as Alice came in the backdoor. "I thought we could work on the Sunrise Room today."

"I'd love to," said Alice.

"Well, I promised Cynthia we'd give her a lesson on faux painting." Jane lowered her voice. "And this way we get some free help too. Who knows, we might even get the painting completed today."

So Jane and Alice and Cynthia spent most of their day happily spreading and wiping layers of pale blue paint on the walls. The floors were already a pickled finish, giving the room a light and airy feel. Alice wanted the room to feel cheerful. Some weeks ago, she had ordered a pretty patchwork quilt from a catalog—a pinwheel pattern in shades of cornflower blue, sunny yellow and a creamy white. They had used this quilt as a guideline for picking paint colors as well as the accessory fabrics that would be used for pillows, curtains and a dust ruffle.

"This room feels happy," said Cynthia after they finished the first wall. "Maybe you'll have a guest who needs to be cheered up and you can put her or him in here."

"Perhaps we should try to define the personalities of the rooms to match the varying needs of our guests," said Alice as she held up a paintbrush.

"The Sunset Room is definitely a very artsy and imaginative room," said Cynthia. "Just staying there makes you want to be more creative."

"That's good," said Jane. "We'll have to remember to write these things down before we forget them."

"Did I hear someone say we need to write things down?" called Louise as she came down the hallway. Then she stuck her head in the bedroom. "Oh, my, girls, that looks lovely."

Cynthia explained their idea to her mother. "Maybe you could put all this in your brochure," she suggested.

"Yes." Louise nodded. "I've been making some notes for these things, and a brief description of the guest rooms would be a nice addition."

"And you'll need a website too," suggested Cynthia as she attempted to remove a blue splotch from the tip of Jane's nose.

"Great idea," said Jane. "I bought the software for creating my own website last year. I wouldn't mind giving it a shot."

"I wonder how I would describe my Symphony Room," said Louise.

"Think about how a symphony makes you feel," suggested Jane as she carefully blotted the narrow wall space between the windows, artistically twisting her rag from left to right.

"Inspired," said Louise.

"Then it should look like an inspiring room," said Cynthia.

Louise frowned. "Well, I hope I picked out the right sort of wallpaper for it then."

"Was that the paper with the rows of climbing roses?" asked Cynthia.

"Yes. Do you think it will feel inspiring at all?"

The bedroom got quiet. "I think so," said Alice after a bit.

"How?" asked Louise with a frown.

Alice paused to refill her brush with paint. "Well, the roses are climbing upward, right?"

"Yes," said Louise. "They are."

"So it sort of inspires you to look up."

"That's right," said Louise. "I think it will be quite uplifting."

"There you go," said Jane.

Louise went back out into the hallway, and then paused.

"But what about Mother's room, Jane? You seem to be keeping your plans for it a secret."

"Yes, Jane," urged Alice. "Don't keep us in suspense."

"Okay." Jane set down her rag and stood up straight. "Naturally, I think that Mother's room will be very gardenlike, with varying shades of green. Very serene and peaceful."

"Peaceful." Louise nodded. "That sounds like Mother."

"Yes," agreed Alice. "I remember how she could make my troubles melt away just by holding me in her arms and stroking my hair."

"That's right," said Louise. "She could simply walk into a room and an air of peace and dignity seemed to accompany her."

Jane sighed sadly. "I wish I had known her."

Alice went over and put an arm around her shoulders. "Don't worry, Jane, you already do."

"I do?"

Alice smiled. "Yes. There is so much of Mother in you, Jane. Of the three of us, you look the most like her."

"Really? You think so?"

"Oh, everyone knows that, Jane," said Louise in a slightly impatient tone. "Father always said you looked just like Mother. And you've seen the photos."

"I guess I just didn't really notice."

"So, if you're ever missing Mother, just take a look in the mirror," said Alice. "You'll get a little peek of her in there."

"All right." Jane straightened her shoulders. "I guess we should get back to work, crew. That is unless we want to be here all night."

"I thought I could fix dinner tonight," offered Louise. "After all the fancy Christmas food we've been eating, I've been hankering after some of my corn chowder."

"Sounds good," said Jane as she winked at Alice.

"*Sounds good?*" repeated Cynthia after her mother was well out of earshot. "Have you guys ever tasted that stuff?"

Alice laughed. "Oh, you'd be surprised, Cynthia. I'm sure it's not nearly as bad as you remember."

Chapter Twenty-Four

$\mathcal{B}$y the New Year, Aunt Ethel had finally managed to completely squelch Florence and Clara's rumor. Alice suspected it took a great deal of effort on her aunt's part, because she knew how gossip could fly through their small town. She had already heard, through Hope, that people were talking about the three sisters' methods of funding their home improvements.

It required someone as well connected and socially active as Aunt Ethel to put a real stop to something like that. Fortunately it seemed that she had succeeded. The down-side was that most of the town was now fully aware of the Howard sisters' financial situation, including how Louise's deceased husband Eliot had been such a savvy investor.

"I hear that Louise's husband made a killing in the stock market before he died," said Hope as she set a piece of blackberry pie in front of Alice. She winked. "Now, who would've dreamed that Louise had actually been married to the Wolf of Wall Street?"

Alice thought about Eliot's thoughtful and modest

personality and just shook her head. "Oh, I wouldn't describe him like that, Hope. Honestly, he was just a nice, quiet man who had fairly good sense when it came to investments."

Hope leaned forward with interest. "So is Louise really a millionaire?"

Alice blinked. "No, not at all."

Hope frowned. "Shoot, I thought it'd be fun to have a real millionaire in town." She glanced around the Coffee Shop. "Everyone says that Hank McPheeter is pretty wealthy, maybe even a millionaire, but I have my doubts."

"Why's that?"

"First off, you should see how he tips." Hope shook her head dismally.

"Maybe that's why he's so well off."

"Guess I'd rather be poor and generous than rich and stingy."

Alice grinned. "I'm with you there."

"So what's going on with the inn these days?"

"Not too much at the moment. Our contractor hasn't come back from the West Coast yet."

"*Hmm.* That Jim ... I can't quite figure him out."

"How's that?"

"Oh, I don't know." Hope shrugged. "I just don't get the feeling that he really likes it here that much."

"What makes you think that? I've only heard him say positive things about Acorn Hill."

"I guess it's just the way he comes across sometimes. Sort of disconnected, you know, like he won't be sticking around for long. I've kind of gotten a sense about these things over the years. I can usually guess which of the newcomers is going to stay."

By the end of the week, Alice wondered if perhaps Hope was right. It was the second week of January, and Jim still hadn't returned from his holiday trip. Jane and Louise were both getting a little worried.

"Do you think he's okay?" asked Louise over dinner one night.

"I wonder if there's someone we should contact," said Jane. "Perhaps we should try to call his son."

"Do you know his son's number?" asked Alice.

"No, but his last name is probably Sharp like his dad's. I could call information and ask."

"I'm sure glad that I didn't pay him any more advance yet," said Louise with a frown. "Then I'd really be worried."

"What if he's sick or has been hurt?" asked Jane. "Wouldn't you be worried then?"

"Well, of course." Louise set down her knife.

"I really wanted to work on the foyer," said Jane. "I feel pretty stuck without Jim's help."

"And the plumbing on the second floor is still at a complete halt," said Alice.

"Oh, he'll probably be back any day now," said Louise. "Let's not worry about it, girls."

"Yes," agreed Alice. "It would be better to just pray."

That night before Alice went to bed, she did remember Jim Sharp in her prayers. "Dear heavenly Father," she prayed, "I ask that You protect Jim and keep him safe. I also ask that You help him to see that You have all the answers for his life's questions. Show him how much You love him, and please . . ." she wondered if this part was selfish, but continnued anyway, "please help him to hurry back to Acorn Hill so that he can finish the inn on time. Amen."

In less than a week, Jim was back on the job. He explained to the three of them that his son's family had all suffered a bad bout of the flu right after Christmas. "And after I helped them to get better, I ended up coming down with it myself."

"Well, we're just relieved that you're okay," said Jane as she handed him a mug of hot coffee.

"And glad that you're back to complete our inn," said Louise.

"Do you have any idea when we'll be up and running?" asked Alice as she reached for her coat. She was already a bit late for work, but she wanted to hear what was going on before leaving.

"Yes," said Jane. "We'd like to be able to announce an opening date for the inn. I'm creating a website, and Louise is having brochures made."

Jim's brow creased as he considered this. "Well, we're closing in on the end of the interior projects. Then we've got the fire escape and meeting the safety codes for the inn. I expect we'll wrap that up by mid-February."

"And pass our final inspections?" asked Louise.

He nodded. "Yep."

"That means we could actually open around Valentine's Day," said Louise happily. "Maybe we could offer some sort of introductory offer for a romantic getaway."

"Oh, that's a good idea," said Jane. "I could bake special desserts and do flowers and—"

"But what about the roof?" asked Alice. "Will that be done by then?"

"No way," said Jim. "I can't even start that up until March." He looked at the date on his watch. "That reminds me, ladies, it's time to order up that slate now. It takes about six weeks to deliver."

"So, does that mean you'll be working on the roof after the inn is running?" asked Alice. "That doesn't sound too safe for the guests."

He waved his hand. "Oh, don't worry about that. There are ways to do these things without upsetting your guests."

Alice wasn't so sure, but she decided not to fret about this as she hurried off to the hospital. More and more, her motto was becoming to pray about everything and worry about nothing. She felt that she had been getting better at it. Father would be proud.

By the end of the week, the foyer wallpaper had been hung, and all three sisters agreed that the pale gold and ivory stripes looked absolutely perfect.

"I feel a little guilty about monopolizing Jim's time these past couple days," admitted Jane. "But I just felt that we needed to get this done."

"I agree wholeheartedly," said Louise. "I've gotten so weary of explaining to everyone that we haven't had a chance to finish it yet. And, of course, it's the first thing people see when they come inside."

"Oh, it's such a welcoming sight," said Alice. "I'm glad that you did it."

"Jim did get all the fire alarms up, and he promised that he'll start on the second-floor bathrooms first thing next week," said Jane.

"And he's ordered the slate now," said Louise. "So everything is right on track for our opening date."

"Just think," said Alice. "We could have real guests in just a month's time."

"Not a moment too soon either," said Louise. "We are

really going to need that income before long. Jim's final check pretty much cleared out our bank account."

"But that will cover absolutely everything left, right?" asked Alice with a wave of concern.

"Yes." Louise sighed. "Mostly it's for the slate. Jim has guaranteed that everything will be completely finished."

"Oh, I can't wait," said Jane. "I think I'll work on my website tonight. I want to get it up and running and see if we can't get some guests lined up for the latter half of February."

"Are you certain that you really want to book guests before we're absolutely sure?" asked Alice. "I mean we can't open our doors without those inspections and—"

"Don't worry, Alice. Jim says it's a piece of cake," Louise assured her.

"Besides, it's a whole month away still," Jane waved her hands at the freshly papered walls. "And just look at this, Alice. Doesn't it make you feel like we're almost there?"

Alice smiled. "Yes, it's very encouraging!"

During the weekend, the three of them worked together on the Garden Room. Jane had completed faux painting the walls in soothing shades of pale green and then added a couple of delicate floral borders above the cherry wood wainscoting and at the ceiling. The sisters had decided to leave their mother's original rosewood bedroom furniture in this bedroom.

"It looks perfect in here," said Alice after they had put everything back into place.

"Yes," agreed Louise. "It goes so well with the wainscoting, plus it really stands out nicely against those pale greens. I do love green, Jane. I'm so glad you decided to go with that in here."

"And it does feel peaceful, doesn't it?" asked Jane.

"Definitely," said Alice. "I feel as if I'm in a garden."

Jane laughed. "It actually makes me want to go find my spade and get my hands dirty. I can't wait to start working up the old garden this spring."

As if to torture Jane, the weather had turned cold and brutal with nearly a foot of snow by Monday. Schools were closed, and the already slow pace in Acorn Hill ground nearly to a halt. Still, people were happy and cheerful as they shoveled their walks and greeted their neighbors.

"Haven't seen s-snow like this since b-back in the eighties," called Pastor Ley as he shoveled the sidewalk in front of the chapel.

"Isn't it beautiful?" Alice called back as she scraped the snow off her car's windshield. She paused to look at the town now draped in a blanket of pristine white. The houses looked so quaint and cozy, and the street lamps wore white caps on their heads.

He nodded as he walked over and started to give a hand

helping her to clear off her car. "S-snow's kind of like God's m-mercy, don't you think? M-makes everything look all clean and white."

Alice laughed. "But thank goodness, God's mercy doesn't melt away."

There were more casualties than usual at the hospital that day, mostly resulting from the weather. A sledding accident yielded a broken collarbone, and a slipping mishap left Viola Reed with a badly sprained ankle.

"How are you feeling, Viola?" asked Alice as she popped into the emergency room to check on her friend.

Viola groaned. "Just wishing these pain pills would kick in."

"Do you need a ride home later today?"

"Thanks, I already asked Donna to close up the shop and come get me. I told her to load me up a box of the newest books to take home with me—might as well catch up on my reading while I'm down."

"You be sure to call if you need any help," said Alice. "And keep that foot iced and elevated."

"Thanks."

Later in the day, a couple whose car had slid off a Potterston road and smacked into a tree came in. They had just been passing through town and fortunately suffered only minor injuries. But the local hotel was full, and now they had no place to stay. Someone in the ER had told them about Alice's bed and breakfast and the husband, Thomas Redding, sought out Alice during the only break she'd been able to get all day.

She set down her tea. "Yes, I heard about your wreck. Too bad."

"Our car's not looking too great, but it could've been much worse." He rubbed a bandage along his chin. "Seems the hotel in town is full, and I wondered if you might possibly have a room available in your inn tonight. I heard that Acorn Hill's not far away."

She smiled. "I'm sorry, but our inn's not open for business just yet. We're still in the renovation stage."

He frowned. "Our car's getting worked on right now, they're just going to patch it up enough to make it home to New York, but it won't be ready until tomorrow afternoon. Do you have any idea where we could stay around here?"

Alice thought for a moment. "Actually, you could probably stay with us, but we couldn't allow you to pay for a room since we're not even licensed yet. Unfortunately the bathrooms on the guest floor aren't finished yet, but there is one downstairs. Are you and your wife able to climb steps?"

He nodded. "April only suffered a broken wrist and some bruising."

"Has she been released from the hospital yet?"

"The doctor plans to check her again. I heard that it would take a couple more hours still. I guess things got busy here today."

"The weather helped out." She glanced at her watch. "My shift ends at five. If you and your wife would like, I could give you a ride then."

He smiled. "Thank you, we really appreciate it."

So Alice called home and explained about the unexpected guests. "I told him that we couldn't accept money since we're not officially open."

"Oh, don't worry about that," said Jane. "It'll be fun just to pretend that we're running an inn tonight. I'll ask Louise to get their room ready. Tell them that they're welcome to stay for dinner. I'll even whip up something special."

The Reddings appeared to be quite impressed with Grace Chapel Inn. Louise gave them the full tour while Alice changed out of her uniform and Jane put the finishing touches on dinner.

"I feel like we've really discovered something special," said April at dinner. "I hope we can come back and stay when you're officially open and we're not in such bad shape."

"Yes, it's an unfortunate way to get acquainted with our little town," said Louise. "We're not at our best just now."

"Everyone has been so helpful and friendly," said Thomas. "It almost makes me wish we lived in a place like this."

"Yes." April nodded. "So quiet and peaceful—nothing like where we live in New York."

"What room are you staying in tonight?" asked Alice.

"The Garden Room," said April. "Louise explained that it was your mother's room. It's simply lovely."

"I thought they would be comfortable in there," said Louise.

Alice thought it seemed fitting that their first guests were nonpaying customers, strangers who'd experienced misfortune and simply needed a shelter for the night. Father would definitely approve.

The Reddings' car was finished as promised the following day, and April and Thomas assured everyone that they would be coming back to Acorn Hill when the inn was opened.

"I told April about our Valentine's Day special," Louise told Alice at dinner. "And she said she might even surprise her husband by booking it. Apparently it's also their twenty-second wedding anniversary next month."

"They might actually become our first paying customers," said Jane happily.

"And to think it was the snow that brought them to us," said Alice. "Sort of like Mother and Father."

"How's that?" asked Jane.

"Don't you remember the story of how Father's car got stuck in the snow, right out there in front of the house," said Alice. "Turned into a real blizzard, and he was stuck here for several days."

"Good thing," said Jane with a grin. "Gave him plenty of time to fall in love with Mother. So maybe the snow's a good sign for our bed and breakfast too."

"Yes, it seems Grace Chapel Inn has a promising future," said Alice.

"There's only one little problem," said Louise in a quiet but serious voice.

"What's that?" asked Alice as she reached for the butter.

"Well," Louise glanced uncomfortably at Jane. "Jim hasn't come to work on the house during the past two days."

"At first we thought it was just the weather," said Jane quickly. "I mean the town was such a complete mess yesterday, and then we were sort of distracted with our unexpected guests. But it suddenly hit both of us this afternoon that we haven't seen Jim since last Friday."

"He may be still getting over the flu," said Louise hopefully.

"You'd think he'd have called or something," added Jane.

"Do you suppose he's too sick to call?" asked Alice. "Or perhaps he's slipped and injured himself. We've had so many injuries related to the snow and ice during these past two days."

"Oh dear, I hope he's okay," said Jane.

"Doesn't he have a phone?" asked Alice. "Can't you call him?"

"We don't have a number."

"Oh." Alice frowned. "Do you know where he lives?"

Louise shook her head. "We've never had any reason to ask him that."

"Maybe Fred knows," said Alice. "They seem to be pretty good friends. I'll call him after dinner."

Alice tried not to worry as she finished her meal. Then she waited until seven to dial up the Humberts' number. Fred told her that Jim lived in the little apartment above the Woods' garage.

"He doesn't have a phone," Fred explained. "I know because I stopped by Time for Tea just last week and asked Wilhelm Wood if he knew anything about Jim. I hadn't seen Jim since before Christmas. I must say I'm sure relieved to hear that he's back in town though."

Alice didn't ask why Fred felt so relieved, but she did dispense this information to her sisters.

"Isn't that out on Village Road?" asked Jane. "Didn't Wilhelm Wood used to live there with his parents?"

"Actually Wilhelm still lives there with his mom," said Alice. "Just the two of them. His dad died a few years back. Their home is just a ways up from the Methodist church. It's a white colonial house with green shutters."

Jane slipped the last plate into the new stainless steel dishwasher and then wiped her hands. "Well, I plan to drive over there first thing tomorrow morning and check on Jim."

"I'll come with you," offered Louise.

"I hope he's all right," said Alice as she hung a pot back on the rack. She had a bad feeling about this.

Chapter Twenty-Five

$\mathscr{A}$lice prayed for Jim as she drove through the melt-ing snow to work the next morning. She prayed for his health and safety—and for his heart. For some reason she couldn't understand, she felt this was especially impor-tant. It was almost time for her lunch break when Jane and Louise stopped by the hospital.

"What are you two doing here?" she asked in a voice that sounded calmer than she felt. She could tell by their expressions that something was seriously wrong.

"We thought we might take you to lunch," said Jane in a stiff voice.

"Sure." Alice forced a smile. "Let me just finish up this paperwork and then I'll get my coat."

Jane drove the three of them over to the Good Apple Bakery and parked the car in front. "They have pretty good soup in here," she said as they all got out and sloshed through the melting slush.

Finally they had ordered their soup and were seated at a quiet corner table. Alice had a cup of hot tea in front of her but she felt chilled on the inside. "Okay, girls," she said. "What's up?"

Louise made a quiet moaning sound, and Jane just shook her head with her eyes downcast.

"Is Jim okay?" asked Alice, suddenly fearful that her sisters might have actually discovered him dead in his bed. Although this seemed unlikely, since she probably would have heard of it at the hospital by now. "Tell me what's wrong."

Jane reached over and took Alice's hand. "He's gone, Alice."

"Gone?" Alice glanced at Louise who now looked close to tears.

Louise nodded. "Gone. Jim is gone."

"We drove over to the Woods' house this morning and knocked on the apartment door," said Jane solemnly. "We waited a good long time, but no one answered."

"Then Mrs. Wood, Wilhelm's mother, came out and asked if she could help us," explained Louise.

"She said she had suspected Jim was gone again and had told her son as much. Apparently Jim's pickup hadn't been around the last few days. She seemed a bit concerned too. Then she got a key and took us back up there and unlocked the apartment. All his personal belongings were gone, Alice. Mrs. Wood told us that Wilhelm might know more about this, but it was plain to see that she was pretty mad."

"So we went ahead and stopped by Time for Tea, and Wilhelm said he didn't know anything about Jim's leaving." Louise nervously fingered her pearls.

"Wilhelm said that he hadn't seen him at all last weekend, but that he'd assumed that Jim was working long hours at our house to catch up after being gone so long." Jane folded and folded her paper napkin until it became a small neat triangle.

"Then Wilhelm told us that Jim still owes him rent from last month and this one too."

"That's not all," said Jane. "We stopped by the hardware store and asked Fred if he knew anything about Jim's sudden departure. He said he hadn't seen him since before Christmas, but that Jim left an unpaid account with him too. I guess it's quite large."

Now Alice knew why Fred had sounded worried last night. She turned back to Louise. "And you already paid him his final advance?"

Louise nodded with a sick expression. "Last Friday."

"But he ordered the slate for our roof, didn't he?" asked Alice hopefully.

Jane just shrugged. "What do you think, Alice?"

"I don't know what to think." She shook her head. "It makes no sense."

"He's left town, Alice," Louise spoke in a flat voice. "He owes people money. What does it look like to you?"

"That he's a thief," said Jane.

"We don't know that for sure," said Alice.

"It doesn't look good," said Jane. "Why would he take off without even calling? Why would he pack all his things and just disappear?"

"We don't even know who to call about the slate either," said Louise. "I never even inquired where he was ordering it from. I suppose I could look in the phone book and just start calling."

Alice looked from one sister to the other. This simply made no sense.

Jane sighed. "Don't waste your time, Louise. I'm betting we won't be seeing that slate anytime soon."

Alice felt tears building in her eyes. "This is just awful. Do you really think that he absconded with the rest of our money?"

"It sure looks like it," said Jane in a tired voice.

"But he seemed like such a capable contractor," said Alice as she dabbed her eyes with her paper napkin. "He was doing such good work, and we weren't even that far from being finished. Why would he do this to us?"

Just then the waitress brought their bowls of soup and bread. She glanced around the table curiously, and then turned and left without saying a word.

"I have absolutely no idea," said Louise. "But I'll tell

you this much. As soon as we get home I'll be doing some phoning and inquiring. His business card has a contractor's license number on it, and I plan to get to the bottom of this before the day is over."

"We won't be able to finish the house now." Jane looked completely dejected as she dipped her spoon in her bowl and then just left it sitting there.

"And we won't be able to open by Valentine's Day," added Louise.

Alice remembered her first impressions of Jim Sharp. For some reason she had never completely trusted the man, but it hadn't been anything she could explain or even put her finger on. She took a couple spoonfuls of the creamy mushroom soup and then pushed her bowl away.

"This is just so wrong," she said. "Are we absolutely sure that he's really left us and taken our money?" She looked at both her sisters. "Maybe his family had a problem, and he had to go back and see them or help out again."

"You really think he'd drive cross-country in his pickup truck in this kind of weather if it were a real emergency?" Jane looked angry now.

"Not to mention packing up and taking all his belongings?" added Louise.

"No." Alice shook her head. "That makes no sense."

"None of this makes sense," said Louise.

"Sometimes life is just like that," said Jane. "Sometimes people can seem perfectly good and then, when you least expect it, they turn around and stab you in the back."

"Oh, Jane." Alice put her hand on Jane's arm. "Even if that's really true. Even if Jim Sharp is nothing more than a thief . . . well, we just can't let something like this completely defeat us."

Jane laughed, but not with humor. "I don't see how we can help it, Alice."

Louise groaned. "I suppose we could consider calling that real estate developer. I think I still have his card. Maybe he could take the house off our hands."

"Louise!" Alice felt shocked. "You can't just give up."

"Our money is gone, Alice." Louise spoke in a tired voice. "We can't afford to finish fixing the house. And we certainly can't open the inn in the condition it's in. The roof is already starting to leak again, and getting it replaced was our biggest expense. It's over."

"I'll go back to working full-time," offered Alice.

Louise shook her head. "That's not going to make up the difference, Alice. Not in time anyway."

"Louise is right," agreed Jane. "It's over, Alice."

"No." Alice firmly shook her head. "It's not over until God says it's over."

Jane rolled her eyes. "Look, Alice, I really think God is telling us it's over."

But Alice was unconvinced. During the next few days, she prayed and prayed that God would redeem their desperate situation. Somehow she maintained a brave front even though she felt as if she were faltering on the inside, because she knew as well as anyone that their situation did appear totally and utterly bleak.

Despite Louise's best efforts to track down Jim Sharp and get some sort of recompense for their losses, it looked hopeless. It turned out that his contractor's license had expired several years ago, and besides that he already had a number of unhappy customers who had filed previous claims against his non-existent bond insurance.

"That man really was a complete scoundrel," she told Jane and Alice later that week.

"Sounds like a professional rip-off artist," said Jane. "A scam man. I've seen news shows on guys like that, but I never thought I'd have a run-in with one."

Alice looked around the interior of the partially renovated house. "But he did actually know about repairing old houses. He did good work."

Jane rolled her eyes. "He's still a thief, Alice."

"I spoke to Fred about Jim's unpaid bill," continued Louise. "I felt as if it was partially our fault since the materials he'd purchased had been used in our home."

Alice nodded. "It'll take us a while to pay him back."

"Well, that's one of the few pieces of good news." Louise sighed. "Fred said that it was between him and Jim and that he had insurance for this type of thing. The truth is Fred feels partially responsible for the whole nasty business."

"Well, he should," snapped Jane. "He was the one who introduced us to Jim in the first place."

"Yes, but it was *our* decision," Alice reminded her.

"You were against it from the start," said Jane sadly. "Why didn't we listen to you, Alice?"

Alice just shrugged. "Doesn't matter now."

"But why was that?" demanded Louise. "How did you know that he was no good, Alice?"

"I don't even know. It just worried me that so much money was involved. I wanted to be certain he was on the up-and-up, but I wasn't sure how to go about it. Once Jim started working, well, I thought perhaps my fears had been foolish."

"But they weren't." Jane shook her head.

"I stopped by Nine Lives this morning," said Alice, hoping to change the subject to something more positive. "I wanted to see how Viola was doing with her ankle, and it looks like she's making a good recovery. She's already back at work."

"Good for her," said Louise without enthusiasm.

"Viola showed me a new section of books she just started carrying." Alice held up a large paperback book. "It's a how-to on plumbing."

"You've *got* to be kidding," said Louise.

Alice shook her head. "Nope. I flipped through it, and it doesn't really look all that complicated. There are lots of helpful drawings and diagrams. I think I might actually be able to hook up those bathroom fixtures upstairs."

Jane laughed. "Oh, Alice. Don't be ridiculous."

"Well, I have the next few days off and I plan to give it my best try."

"Okay, then," said Jane with unexpected determination. "If you're sure you want to tackle this, I'll do whatever I can to help you."

Alice smiled. "Let's just hope that that old saying is true."

"What's that?" asked Louise as she set aside her knitting and rubbed her forehead.

"You know what Ben Franklin said: God helps those who help themselves."

"*Humph.*" Louise shook her head grimly. "Like that rascal Jim Sharp who helped himself to our money?"

"You know that we have to forgive him," Alice reminded her.

"Not today, I don't." Louise stood up and smoothed her skirt. "Today I have to give music lessons. And if you and old Ben are right, if God really does help those who help themselves, then I better get busy."

So with Louise's young students plunking on the piano

downstairs, Alice and Jane started plunking on the plumbing upstairs, and by the end of the day Sarah Roberts could play "Twinkle, Twinkle, Little Star," and one toilet was actually hooked up and operable.

The three sisters sat down to a dinner of leftovers and laughter.

"Well," said Louise after telling them about several of her less than gifted pupils, "if we somehow manage to weather this storm, I'm sure we'll be better people for it in the long run."

"Not to mention plumbers," added Alice.

"I hear plumbers make pretty good money," said Jane.

Still, this didn't address the issue of their leaking roof. The recent heavy snow and thaw and refreezing had created several new leaks in the attic. Alice had rounded up some more buckets from the basement and emptied them as needed, but she knew this wouldn't solve their problem for long.

Chapter Twenty-Six

*T*hanks to Aunt Ethel, it wasn't long before every citizen in Acorn Hill and half the county had heard the story of the sticky-fingered contractor.

"Just goes to show you," said Lloyd Tynan at a church board meeting. "Better watch out for those outsiders."

"That's right," agreed Florence Simpson in her I-told-you-so voice. "I wouldn't dream of hiring an outsider to work on my house."

"Well, fact is, we were all outsiders at one time," said Fred.

"Not me," said Lloyd proudly. "I was born and raised in Acorn Hill."

"So was I," said Fred. "But that's not what I mean."

"You mean our ancestors," said Florence. "Well, I happen to be third generation in this town."

"Look," Fred continued. "My family has been here for generations too, but at one point they were the outsiders—the newcomers."

"I suppose you're right about that," said Lloyd with a thoughtful nod.

After the meeting ended and they were having cookies and tea, Alice overheard a snippet of conversation between Aunt Ethel and Florence.

"Now, Florence, if this is going to work, you'll need to keep it under your hat." Aunt Ethel had a warning tone to her voice.

Florence huffed. "Well, of course, Ethel. Don't you think I know how to keep a secret?" Just then Aunt Ethel noticed Alice and put her finger to her mouth as if to silence her friend.

"As I was saying," said Florence loudly. "I think it's an absolute shame that Acorn Hill is going to miss out on having an inn."

Alice felt her eyebrows rise and wondered if she hadn't just stepped into the Twilight Zone, but in the next minute the two women were chattering away about Bingo Night. Well, go figure!

It took a couple of weeks, but Jane and Alice, with occasional and much appreciated help from Fred, somehow managed to get the bathrooms on the second floor up and running.

"You girls are really something," said Aunt Ethel as she watched Alice proudly flushing the last toilet.

Alice sighed. "It's an accomplishment all right, but we still have the roof to figure out."

"Goodness." Aunt Ethel's eyes grew wide. "You certainly don't intend to climb up there and replace that slate yourself, now do you?"

"I don't know," said Alice. "If we actually had some slate, I might consider it."

"*Tsk-tsk.* It's just such a shame," Aunt Ethel said.

"It isn't over with yet, Auntie."

"Is there any hope of catching that scallywag and getting your money back?"

Alice shrugged. "It doesn't look like it."

"Too bad." Aunt Ethel looked around the renovated bathroom with approval. "Everything looks so nice too. You girls were so close."

"We haven't given up yet, Aunt Ethel." Alice picked up the tools that were still spread across an old towel on the floor. "Louise is making a little money teaching piano. I'll go back to working full-time next month. Jane is selling her baking to the Coffee Shop. We might be able to get enough money for the roof."

"When?" Aunt Ethel peered at her with obvious skepticism.

Alice forced a smile to her lips. "Oh, in a year or so."

Aunt Ethel shook her head. "Too bad." Then she smiled in a curious way. Alice almost asked her what was so amusing, but then decided perhaps it was better not to know.

Valentine's Day came and went with no possibility of opening the inn anytime soon. Louise had already informed the Reddings that their reservations had to be canceled "due to unforeseen circumstances." Even with the plumbing nearly in order, there was still a myriad of smaller jobs that needed to be completed before their final inspection would be approved, things like a wobbly handrail and a fire exit and some electrical outlets that needed to be replaced. More troublesome than all of that was the general condition of the rapidly deteriorating roof. With heavy rains in February, the attic had turned into what now appeared to be a bucket brigade. Alice and Jane kept a vigilant watch and emptied the buckets regularly, but it was obvious that it was only getting worse.

It was a sunny day in early March when Alice came home from work to see a curious sight in their front yard. Pallets and pallets of what appeared to be roofing material were stacked everywhere. It was not slate, she could tell, but it was definitely some sort of shingle.

She hurried into the house and called for her sisters. "What's going on out there?" she asked when she finally discovered the two them huddled in the small office that Louise had created under the stairway.

"Oh, Alice," said Louise with overly bright eyes. "Have you heard the news?"

"What?" Alice felt her heart leaping with excitement. "Has Jim come back? Did he order those—"?

No," Jane shook her head. "This has *nothing* to do with Jim."

"What then? What's going on?"

"It's the town," said Louise as her eyes overflowed with tears. "They've all been working together these past few weeks. Just everyone—" Her voice broke with the emotion.

"It's unbelievable," said Jane. "We have no idea who organized the effort, but people from all over Acorn Hill have contributed—and generously. Did you know that the hospital even had a secret jar for donations, the hardware store and the Coffee Shop too? Why, just about everyone. Fred said that Vera even got the grammar school involved by having a big bake sale."

"And your ANGELs helped out too," added Louise. "They've been doing yard work around the town and saving every single penny for the Grace Chapel Inn roofing fund."

"Lloyd and Aunt Ethel even talked the chamber into donating some bingo funds," added Jane. "They said it was okay since we'll be an official business in this town before too long and they invited us to join the chamber."

Alice felt her knees going weak as she sat down in the desk chair. "This is so unbelievable."

"Isn't it amazing!" Jane's cheeks were flushed with excitement. "Only six months ago we felt like we were fighting an uphill battle just to get the townsfolk of Acorn Hill to accept the possibility of an inn."

"Now, they're helping to fund it," Louise finished for her as she wiped her nose with a linen handkerchief.

"Not to change the subject, but Fred called just a bit ago," said Jane. Her face grew more serious now. "He said that he spoken to Clark Barrett."

Alice felt a wave of regret as she considered the old trustworthy contractor that they had chosen to bypass in order to hire Jim Sharp. "What did Clark have to say?"

Jane sadly shook her head. "Clark was skeptical of Jim from the start. I guess he'd heard rumors from some of the tradesmen in the area."

"I wish Clark had said something back then," said Louise.

"Perhaps we should've invited Clark for a bid back then," offered Alice weakly.

Louise sighed. "Yes, it's plain to see now that it would've been wise to have gotten a second estimate."

"Anyway," continued Jane, "Fred said that Clark hadn't wanted to interfere, but that he'd heard that Jim might have had some problems."

"Problems?" Louise's brows lifted.

Jane nodded soberly. "Fred said that Clark had heard that Jim had a gambling problem, but at the time he wasn't sure that it was true, so naturally he didn't want to spread a rumor."

Louise shook her head. "Well now, that would explain a thing or two."

"That's too bad," said Alice.

"Yes," agreed Jane. "As angry as I was at Jim, I do feel a bit sorry for him now. It would be awful to not only steal someone else's money but then to have gambled it away too."

"A horrible way to live," said Louise.

"We should keep him in our prayers," suggested Alice.

"You're right," agreed Louise. "After all, God must've brought that man along our path for a reason. We can certainly pray for him."

"Well, on to more pleasant things," said Jane as her face brightened. "Fred said that he and Clark would be organizing a work crew."

"Clark actually wants to help us?" asked Alice.

Jane nodded happily.

"Why, that's wonderful," said Louise.

"Fred said that their crew would be coming by during the next few days to get the old roof torn off and replaced. All we need to do is to feed them." Jane smiled. "I assured him that we could do that with no problem."

"Fred asked what else it would take to get our licensing

approved," said Louise. "So Jane and I gave him the little tour and he said that his crew would take care of those things too."

Alice just shook her head in total amazement. "I feel like I'm dreaming. But, please, don't wake me up."

Louise laughed. "Well, remember what you said about God helping those who help themselves."

She nodded. "I really didn't think God would let us down."

"But isn't it incredible that God is using some of the very people who originally opposed us to help us now?" Jane looked even more stunned than Alice felt.

"Yes." Louise nodded firmly. "Fred said that Florence Simpson even helped out."

"You're kidding?"

"No. Fred said the church board did a little secret fund-raising on its own, and Florence actually oversaw the whole thing. Of course, he said that she expects that the church will get as much support from us when it's time to replace the roof there."

Alice laughed. "Leave it to Florence to use this to another advantage. But that's all right with me. I'll be more than glad to help raise funds for the church's roof."

"So I'm getting ready to send out those brochures now," said Louise.

"And I'm updating our Web site," added Jane.

"There's so much to do," said Louise. "Our goal is to be open by Easter week."

"Goodness, that's only a few weeks away. Are you sure?"

"It's a matter of faith," Jane reassured her.

Alice had to smile to herself to hear Jane speak in such a manner. But then they had all come such a long way during the past six months. And, it seemed, miracles still happened.

For the next week, there were young men and even a few women traipsing through the house, consuming large quantities of food, climbing up and down ladders and scrambling around on the steeply pitched roof. Clark proved extremely useful as he supervised the workers and kept the operation moving like clockwork. There was the constant cacophony of hammers and drills and Louise's piano students plunking away on the piano. But it was a happy sort of noise. It reminded Alice of an old time barn-raising.

By the end of the week, the new roof was completely installed. It wasn't slate, of course, for Fred said that was too expensive, but it was solid and weatherproof and the soft taupe color, picked out by Vera, blended quite nicely with the new paint.

Everyone gathered outside after church on Sunday to visit and admire the work that had been done. And all seemed to agree that the house, the renovations, and even the prospect of the inn were very good things.

"But we have another surprise for you girls," said Aunt Ethel with a knowing grin.

Vera winked at Aunt Ethel. "Don't give it away completely now."

"Don't you worry," said Aunt Ethel. "I just want to make sure they don't have any other plans."

"What are you talking about?" asked Jane.

"We want the three of you to join us in the assembly room at two," said Vera.

"It's a surprise," said Aunt Ethel. "Don't be late."

So at exactly two in the afternoon, Louise, Alice and Jane trekked over to the chapel. They could hear the laughter and twittering of female voices as they went down the stairs.

"Surprise!" yelled the women.

"Why, it looks like a shower," said Alice as she looked around the decorated room in confusion. She spied the white crepe paper bows and bells and all the usual trappings and trimmings that she often put out for a bridal shower. "But who's getting married?"

Patsy Ley laughed. "We don't have to wait for someone to get married to throw a shower, do we girls?" The other churchwomen nodded and happily agreed.

"We wanted to throw a shower for Grace Chapel Inn," said Vera. "A linen shower."

"That is so thoughtful," said Jane.

"What a beautiful idea," agreed Louise. Alice noticed there were tears in her older sister's eyes.

So for the next couple of hours, the three of them took turns opening box after box of sheets and towels and candles and soaps and everything you could ever want for a bed and breakfast.

"But how did you know what to get?" asked Alice when they were finally done.

"It was Vera," admitted Aunt Ethel. "She wrote out the colors of the rooms and bed sizes and bathroom colors and everything."

"Thank you all so much," said Louise. "You have no idea how much this means to us."

Later on that evening, after the sisters had put away their shower gifts, they gathered around Jane's kitchen and shared a pot of orange pekoe tea.

"This town is amazing," said Jane. "Really amazing."

Louise nodded. "Yes, I'll have to admit there were times early on when I wasn't so sure, but these people are truly wonderful."

Alice smiled. "They truly are," she said.

"Do we have everything we need now, Louise?" asked Jane.

"Well, not everything, but we've got enough to make a

respectable start. According to the book I've been reading on bed and breakfasts, we should have at least three sets of sheets per room and enough towels to supply each guest with two sets per day for up to three days."

"Goodness, that seems a lot," said Alice.

"I guess it's so we don't have to do laundry every day," suggested Jane.

"I don't mind doing laundry," said Louise. "In fact, it's always been one of my favorite household chores. Something about the smell of freshly laundered linens always puts me in a good state of mind."

"I've been wondering about a few things," said Jane as she pulled out her little notebook. "I thought I could make special French chocolate mints to put on the pillows each day."

"Sounds delightful," said Alice. "Do we get them too?"

Jane grinned. "And what about putting a basket of goodies in the rooms? Or do you think that's too extravagant?"

"According to my book," said Louise, "each B and B should have its own signature. For instance, Jane's specialty mints and fresh flower arrangements might be ours. I think perhaps we should hold off on the goody baskets to start with. It could become expensive."

"Right," agreed Jane. "We wouldn't want to start a precedent that we couldn't maintain, but maybe we could offer something like that as an extra."

"Yes," said Alice. "That's a good idea. Make baskets available on an individual basis, like for anniversaries or birthdays."

They went through a second pot of tea and several pages of notes before they finally called it a night. As Alice prepared for bed, it occurred to her that what was once only a dream for their bed and breakfast was steadily becoming a reality.

During the following week, Fred was kept busy with his hardware store, but Clark and a smaller crew of Craig Tracy and Wilhelm Wood popped in sporadically to repair a hand railing or work on the fire escape. Wilhelm's area of expertise was electrical and he managed to get everything up and running on the second floor. And always these willing workers were treated with the specialty of the day from Jane's cheerful kitchen.

"I think I should order some of your currant scones for my shop," said Wilhelm as he picked up his second one of the morning. "These are quite remarkable. I think they'd be a hit in Time for Tea."

"I'll hand deliver them to you for two weeks, on the house, of course," offered Jane as she refilled his cup. "As a thank you for your electrical help."

"Have you started working that garden yet, Jane?" asked Craig as he finished up a large cinnamon roll.

"You should see what she's done," bragged Alice as she began making a fresh pot of coffee. "She cleaned out all the weeds and overgrowth and has some raised beds all ready for planting now."

"It's about that time," said Craig. "Come by the shop next week and I'll give you some of those new seeds I told you about."

"Great." Jane smiled. "The ones I started are already doing quite well. I set up a couple of racks in the sunroom and started some vegetable seedlings too. Besides the flowers, I want to have a salad and herb garden too."

"By the way, Alice," said Fred, "Vera said to tell you, that factory outlet outside of Philly is having some fantastic sale on sheets and towels this weekend. She thought you still needed a few things for the inn."

"Yes, there are still a few missing items, but Jane made a list I could give to Vera. Louise says that we've already got rooms booked for Easter week, and even afterward. It's so exciting."

"Well, give Vera a call. She said she was thinking about driving over there this afternoon."

"Thanks, Fred. I will."

"*Yoo-hoo*," called Aunt Ethel from the back porch.

"We're in here," Alice called back. "You're just in time for morning break."

"Don't mind if I do," said Aunt Ethel as she spied the scones. Then she handed Alice a small flat box.

"What's this?"

"Oh, just a little something I picked up for the inn last week." She went to the coffee pot and helped herself to a fresh cup.

Alice opened the box to see a leather bound guest book, soft white with gold letters. "Oh, thank you, Aunt Ethel. We hadn't even thought about this yet."

"Well, I figured you'd need it to keep track of all your guests." Aunt Ethel sat down next to Fred at the table and picked up a scone. "It might come in handy for Louise to make some sort of mailing list."

"So you're not worried about all that traffic coming and going in the neighborhood these days?" teased Fred.

Aunt Ethel waved her hand. "Goodness, no. How much traffic could there be with only four guest rooms? It's not as if they'll all be full seven days a week."

"I hope not," said Alice. "That might wear us out. Our goal is just to stay busy enough to keep the place going."

"Besides," said Aunt Ethel. "It'll be fun meeting some new folks. Might even liven things up around this old one-horse town."

Chapter Twenty-Seven

lice stopped by the cemetery after she finished her shift on Good Friday. She had considered inviting her sisters to join her but knew they were busy getting the inn ready to open the following day. She felt a tiny wave of guilt as she walked toward the family plot—perhaps she should be home helping them. Yet it seemed important to do this right now. Good Friday had always been one of Father's favorite days. He had loved commemorating the significance of what Jesus had given on the cross—a gift of mercy and love and grace.

Alice set the bouquet of lilies, tulips and daffodils between the graves of her two parents and stepped back. "I realize that you're both in heaven now," she said in a quiet voice. "But somehow I feel I can think and even speak more clearly out here." She leaned her head back and looked at the clear blue sky. "I hope that you both like what we've done with the family home. I think that you've both had a hand in it."

She shoved her hands into the pockets of her uniform and sighed. "I mean, when I consider the amazing way that

things have been working out for us . . . well, it just seems
that someone must be putting in a good word for us up
there. Anyway, I just want to thank you both for being such
great parents and for giving me such wonderful sisters. I'll
bet you've been smiling up there, Father, to see your three
girls finally working together like this. I think it's what you
were hoping for before you left us down here to carry on."
Then Alice bowed her head and thanked God for His perfect plan, for His impeccable timing and, of course, for His
truly amazing grace. Satisfied, she climbed back into her car
and drove home to Grace Chapel Inn.

The three sisters worked together all evening in prepa-
ration for the official inn-opening ceremonies scheduled
for the following morning. Aunt Ethel stopped by and gave
Louise a hand in frosting the dozens of hot cross buns that
Jane had been baking for most of the day. Meanwhile, Jane
was busily designing beautiful floral arrangements, one for
every room. Craig Tracy had given her a generous discount
on blooms with the expectation that she would pay him
back in kind when her garden began to produce in abun-
dance. Already many of the bulbs were blooming and the
pruned rosebushes showed promise, and the grounds
around the house looked almost as attractive as when
Mother was alive. In time, Alice expected they would look
even better. And that was okay.

"What do you think of this one?" asked Jane as she held up a lovely crystal vase filled with purple lilacs, baby's breath, white roses and fresh sprigs of ivy.

"Oh, that's beautiful," said Louise as she paused from her frosting chore.

"I thought it should go in the parlor," said Jane. "Perhaps on your piano, Louise?" She held up a lace doily with a grin.

"On a doily, Jane?" asked Louise with an expression of mock horror. "You would actually allow a lace doily in Grace Chapel Inn?"

Jane nodded. "Yes, I think it would go well in the parlor."

Alice giggled as she polished Mother's old silver coffee set. "Times, they are a-changing, Louise."

Jane laughed. "We've come a long way, baby."

"What do you mean?" asked Aunt Ethel, unsure of the context of the joke.

"Just that change is good," said Jane.

Aunt Ethel's chins jiggled as she nodded vigorously. "I couldn't agree more. When I think of all the wonderful changes that have come around this old house during the past year . . . well, it just makes me so proud of you three girls."

Alice smiled to remember how resistant Aunt Ethel had been to their plans only six months ago. But like the weather she too had changed.

"It's so thoughtful of you girls to invite the whole town to your grand opening tomorrow," she continued, in happy oblivion to the glances that Jane and Alice were exchanging just now.

"It's the least we can do to say thank you," said Louise as she carefully applied another confectionary cross to a currant bun.

"Yes," said Jane as she began artfully to arrange some yellow rosebuds and blue hyacinths together in a smaller vase. Alice was guessing that this cheerful little bouquet might be for the Sunrise Room. "We wouldn't be having a grand opening without the town's generous help."

"And it was so nice of you to invite Lloyd to give a little speech," said Aunt Ethel.

Alice chuckled. "Can you imagine having an event like this without a few words from our beloved mayor?"

"Well, no. That wouldn't be very kind, now would it?"

"When is Cynthia coming?" asked Alice.

"She said she'll be here in time for the ceremony tomorrow," said Louise. "I told her that she's staying in the Sunrise Room."

"Did she mind?" asked Alice. "I know how she loved the Sunset Room, but it was already booked."

"Not all," said Louise. "She said she needed some cheering up."

"Why's that?" asked Aunt Ethel. "Something wrong with our girl?"

"I'm afraid it has to do with her love life," said Louise. "Naturally, she wouldn't tell me a thing. Although I'm hoping that Jane might get her to talk."

"I think the Sunrise Room is just what Cynthia needs," said Jane as she held up the finished bouquet. "This is going to go on the dresser up there."

"You're making this into such a lovely place," said Aunt Ethel. "What if people never want to go home?"

Louise laughed. "Well, then I guess we'll never have to worry about booking rooms, will we?"

"Not that it's been much of a problem," said Jane. "We're starting to get requests for next fall already."

"Amazing." Aunt Ethel shook her head. "You girls may have really stumbled onto something with this inn business."

Chapter Twenty-Eight

A crowd of nearly a hundred people gathered outside of Grace Chapel Inn the following morning. Earlier, Jane had tied a large purple ribbon across the front of the porch, and Aunt Ethel was equipped with a giant pair of scissors that had been borrowed from City Hall the previous day.

Lloyd Tynan opened the ceremony with an eloquent speech about how important it was for the community to support local businesses. "Our local businessmen and women are the backbone of Acorn Hill," he continued as he drew his oration to an end. "We can all understand and appreciate how well-managed establishments like Grace Chapel Inn will benefit the entire town. It is with great pride and pleasure that I welcome this fine business to our fair city today. But before I cut the ribbon, the owners of the inn have invited Pastor Ley to ask a special blessing. I give you Pastor Ley."

Pastor Ley made his way to the top of the porch steps and adjusted his collar and then cleared his throat. "Uh, if we could all . . . just b-bow our heads."

Alice breathed a silent prayer that Pastor Ley would not stammer too badly this morning.

"Dear heavenly Father, we honor You t-today with the opening of this inn. We ask that You b-bless every room with Your presence, that You give strength and w-wisdom to the owners, that You pour out refreshment and rest upon each guest, and that You b-bless the entire place with Your unconditional love and m-merciful grace. Amen."

Lloyd echoed a hearty amen, then held up the oversized sheers. "Ladies and gentlemen, I give you Grace Chapel Inn." Then he sliced through the ribbon, and Alice, Louise and Jane greeted their well-wishers and welcomed them into the inn.

"There are refreshments in the dining room," said Aunt Ethel with a big smile. "I helped make them myself."

Soon the inn was full of people wandering from room to room, *oohing* and *aahing* and making positive comments.

"I can't wait to have my daughter and son-in-law visit again," said Ellen Moore. "I'll put them up here. So much better than having to move all of my sewing things out of the guest room."

Even Florence and Clara showed up, and fortunately Alice didn't overhear them making any slanderous comments this time. In fact, she actually heard Clara telling Viola Reed that she thought Jane should consider going into full-time interior design. "I hear they did this whole inn on a shoestring," said Clara in a hushed voice.

Alice had to suppress her laughter as she exited into the kitchen to remind one of her ANGELs, on hand to help out, to remember to refill the coffee pot.

"Is Mrs. Smith going to play piano today?" asked Sarah Roberts.

"She is," promised Alice. "Make sure you get a chance to go listen when she does. I hear that your lessons are going well, Sarah."

Sarah's eyes shone. "Really? Did Mrs. Smith really say that?"

Alice smiled as she refilled the silver tray with more hot cross buns. "Don't say that you heard it from me though."

"May I help you, Aunt Alice?" asked Cynthia as she poked her head in the kitchen.

"No, I'm just bringing this out," said Alice. "I think the ANGELs have it pretty much under control."

"I love the Sunrise Room," she whispered.

Alice's eyes lit up. "Really? I know it isn't nearly as beautiful as the Sunset Room that Jane designed, but you probably already heard that your mother had booked it with the Ashton couple from Maine."

Cynthia shook her head. "You shouldn't compare the rooms, Aunt Alice. It's like comparing oranges and apples—

or aunts for that matter. Each is lovely in a special way. When I took my bags up there earlier, before the ceremony began, I immediately began to feel happier."

Alice gave her niece a sideways hug. "Oh, I'm so glad. I wanted it to be a happy room, to cheer people up."

Cynthia laughed. "Just like you do!"

The grand opening ceremony ended at eleven, giving everyone—including the ANGELs, Aunt Ethel and Cynthia—a chance to get things tidied up before the first guests began to arrive. Even Vera stuck around to help.

"Thought you could use a hand," she said as she took the broom from Alice and started sweeping the foyer.

"Thanks, Vera." Alice bent over to pick up a piece of pastry that was stuck to the floor. "I just hope none of the guests shows up early."

"If they come early, just hand them a mop."

Alice laughed. "Yeah, that's a sure way to guarantee return guests."

"Or guarantee that they don't show up early."

But everything was back in its place by noon, and the first guests didn't even arrive until nearly one—a young couple from Pittsburgh. All four rooms would be booked on their first official night of business, and three of them with paying guests. And the Ashtons from Maine planned to stay on for the entire week!

"I feel like I'm playing house," said Louise as the three sisters gathered in the kitchen to discuss the day's events.

"What do you think of the Grants?" asked Jane as she poured a cup of tea.

"They seem very sweet," said Alice. "Did you know the wife is expecting?"

"Really? I thought they were newlyweds," said Louise.

"No, she said they'd been married a few years now. But this is their first child and she's feeling a little nervous." Alice helped herself to a leftover hot cross bun.

"I'm curious about the Ashtons," said Jane. "They're staying here all week. Is it just for a rest?"

"Her grandparents used to live in Acorn Hill," said Louise. "I went to school with her mother—Susanna Webb—do you remember her, Alice?"

"Just vaguely."

"Apparently she passed away last year, and the daughter is taking a sentimental journey to help her through it."

"That's sweet," said Jane. "It must be hard not to know where your parents came from. I guess we're fortunate to have all our family history right here at our fingertips."

"What happened to Cynthia?" asked Alice. "I haven't seen her all afternoon."

"Didn't you know?" said Jane with a twinkle in her eye.

"She's in the parlor chatting with the nice young man who booked the Garden Room."

"That's Thomas Moore," said Louise. "Nice looking fellow."

"I must admit that I wondered why you gave him that room," said Alice. "I figured you would save the largest room for couples."

"Well, he was the first one to call and make a reservation," explained Louise. "And he did ask for our best room."

"He seems nice," said Jane. "He has his own business and can take it on the road wherever he goes. Apparently he doesn't have much family to spend holidays with though. He said he felt right at home here."

"I think he's helping Cynthia to forget about whatever it was that was troubling her before she got here," added Louise.

"So all is well at Grace Chapel Inn." Alice sighed with contentment.

"The fun has just begun," said Jane with a twinkle in her eye.

"Not to mention the work," said Louise. "Not that I'm complaining, mind you. Nothing wrong with an honest day's work."

Alice looked around the cozy kitchen and smiled at her little family. "And God is at home here."

Tales from Grace Chapel Inn™

Back Home Again
by Melody Carlson

Recipes & Wooden Spoons
by Judy Baer

Once you visit the charming village of Acorn Hill, you'll never want to leave. Here, the three Howard sisters reunite after their father's death and turn the family home into a bed and breakfast. They rekindle old memories, rediscover the bonds of sisterhood, revel in the blessings of friendship, and meet many fascinating guests along the way.

Melody Carlson is the author of numerous books for children, teens, and adults—with sales totaling more than two million copies. She has two grown sons and lives in central Oregon with her husband and chocolate Lab retriever.